# Mr. Big's Magickal Guide to Gambling

Georgia Liberty and Wayne Clingman

Published by Georgia Liberty, 2024.

MR. BIG'S MAGICKAL GUIDE TO GAMBLING

**First edition. April 15, 2024.**

Copyright © 2024 Georgia Liberty and Wayne Clingman.

ISBN: 979-8224930418

Written by Georgia Liberty and Wayne Clingman.

Dedication From Mr. Big

To Saint Cajetan: Thank you for helping me gamble on growing old. I am cashing out on time, but I am thankful for your help in taking on the challenge.

To Heather Ferris Because.


Dedication From Georgia Liberty

To my husband and my girls, magick is all around you.

# Foreword

From Mr. Big:

In my book section, I will show you a few tricks to make your stay at the Casino more fun and help your bankroll last longer. These tricks are helpful, but they will need Your help to overcome the power of the mathematical statistics of gaming odds, for in the long run, the odds favor the house. If you think that any system will overcome your senses or make you uncomfortable, it is best to stay away from those topics. Please consider other manners you agree with.

I acknowledge that there may be disagreement over more than a few tricks and the like, which I will reference. I am doing this based on what I was taught or discovered from my research. Your discoveries are just as valid as mine. NOTE: This is for entertainment purposes only.

The lot is cast into the lap, but every decision is from the LORD. Proverbs 16:33

Farmers who wait for perfect weather never plant. If they watch every cloud, they never harvest. Ecclesiastes:114

Let us begin

# Preface

From Mr. Big:

As a child, I would go with my mom to visit my great Aunt, an older woman who used to take care of her Herb Garden and make Raisin Jack by the gallon. From time to time, neighbors would come over and talk to my Aunt, who would give the neighbor a few herbs or cuttings, sometimes bring out a small vile along with some discussion, and they would be on their way. On a Saturday visit, well-dressed men stop by, and my Aunt would give them what I thought were Coin Purses; the man give my Aunt a wad of bills since my Uncle injured from a work injury was unable to do much the Cash along with the Herbs she grew, then would sell help a lot, my Uncle I later found out would sell the Raisin Jack around the area they lived in. If you have drank MD 20/20, you come close; in fact, Jack is far, far worse. When I was a bit older, my Aunt would start to teach me a bit about gardening, like why she planted three seeds in the first row of each crop she platted, what phase of the moon it was best to plant in, why she named her scarecrow and talked to it when in the garden, and that it was vital to leave out a bit of milk once in awhile in the kitchen. About 8 or 9, we moved away; shortly after that, after my aunt passed, my uncle started to suffer from dementia. Once we moved away from the Rock Springs area, I was discouraged from talking about my unit, gardening tips, or, God forbid, reciting the rhymes I knew, or worse, asking questions about them. Life goes on. After the army, I ran into college kids practicing Wicca. Studying that and folklore at U.W. Madison,

I discovered that my kin was practicing Hoodoo/Root Magic, which runs deep on my mother's side. Researching Hoodoo's history in the urban centers of the north, I found out a lot about my kin and God and how they made a living practicing that. As you may know, I write books on the Mafia and a few on Vegas table games. In doing so, I discovered the uses of Root Magic not only in policy games (numbers) but in daily life, where luck, spiritual protection, and a bit of reeducation via a Hex could be the difference between life and death in the eyes of us (and I will include myself) who are willing to see a world that others are blind to.

# Acknowledgement

Big thank you and shout out the cover artist, and the readers.

Without you, we wouldn't be here.

# Introduction

Have you ever wondered why fewer people use magick when they gamble than in any other aspect of their lives? Do you think influencing cosmic vibrations is forbidden or completely impossible? Are you a gamer looking to add an extra boost to your gambling strategy? Mr. Big's Magickal Guide to Gambling is an excellent place for any occult-oriented gambler to start learning about the history and relationships between people and the magickal realm when they want to build a sound rationale for implementing magick into their gambling strategy. This guide will be crucial for gaining a firm foundation of understanding the origins of gambling, numerology, lucky charms, potions, rituals, and human nature. Our volume includes a vast knowledge of standard gaming practices, well-known magickal lore, items that can be used for luck, and famous names from many recorded eras in time known for practicing numerology and astronomy for prosperity. Referenced throughout the pages, we will work to illustrate how a variety of techniques were developed in history to utilize magick in gambling in every arena and how they can still be used for your gambling strategy, too. We labored through the literature to ensure our book contains an in-depth bibliography section backing up our research for your quick reference convenience. In addition to citing our sources, we wanted to include a section dedicated to asking for help with a severe addiction, magickal or otherwise. We went as far as to give you direct links to where you can receive access to confidential or group therapy if required. Everything you'll need to get started on your winning streak is at your fingertips.

With this guide, from the first shuffle of the page to the next turn of the river, you'll be betting on your own will against the odds of the gamble. Your charms will be extra lucky, the mojo will be dominantly strong, and people will be drawn to your compelling vibe. Learn where to find winning numbers in the stars and why it matters what you have for dinner before you make that first bet. Read about the inherent success of recording and crafting a magickal strategy for gambling. Then take your magick into the casino. Our pocket-size manual makes it simple to keep this book in your pocket for quick access whenever needed. It is easily digestible yet remains packed with solid material suitable for any appetite of intellect, whether you prefer to expound or minimize your techniques. Size and performance matter; therefore, we made a concise, straight-to-the-point text so anyone can relate their personal belief system with a magickal method that achieves their gambling needs. You will not need to waste time with strategies that peg you for an 'ABC' player when you know you have an ace up your sleeve or a clump of graveyard moss in your pocket.

Our magickal manners of gaining wealth and prosperity, invoking positive vibrational energy, and predicting the winning combinations of patterns while gaming have been proven to withstand the test of time. The history section of our manual enshrines those who made a living studying and teaching the positive effects of humans interacting metaphysically with their environment. Civilization, magick, and gambling grew alongside each other throughout the ages, cajoling the entwinement of body, soul, and environmental effects. People can't escape their ties to the universe, so we teach you how to enjoy it. Magick can be employed by whoever is willing to learn from the past, present, and future. Let us show you where it started, how you can make it your own, and how it can change your fortune. We can tell you how ancient people actually regarded gaming and gambling endeavors, revealing a deeper meaning behind popular casino entertainment today. What we have in store will immediately resign you to constructing your ritual for success.

After you finish Mr. Big's Magickal Guide to Gambling, you'll be running the tables in no time. With the confidence you'll gain from using a magickal gambling technique you believe in, a winning atmosphere will follow you everywhere. Read about the foundations of gambling and human civilization. Expand your knowledge of crafting magickal spells and charms and obtain access to the most personal forms of putting together practical gambling aids. Understand where to find profitable planetary alignments and advantageous number sequences, and familiarize yourself with why magick is often categorized as fickle or ineffectual. You'll even get all the tips and tricks to help you troubleshoot if things go wrong. Once you know the secret to sense the vibrational energy of others, you'll push your chips all in on your personally significant magickal gambling strategy, tilting the tables on your opponents. Keep reading to be adequately equipped to find your next winning magickal combination and make confident strategy recommendations to others based on historical facts. Don't waste any more time losing, being an ADT for the casino, and overpower the House edge today. Control your hot streaks and have peace of mind, knowing that the odds are in your favor. Take your level of play from beginner to shark now. What are you waiting for?

Our manual will be your go-to gambling guide, period. The chapters of our book incorporate the history of a broad range of sincerely held belief systems of the people of Earth from the decades and explain how they grew and expanded the art of profiting from the use of magick. Everyone observed a unique gambling method from the top to the bottom of the social ladder. Compare your lucky rituals to those of famous scholars, kings, and folklore superstitions. Track and construct individualized stepping stones taken directly from the universe to lay down for your path to winning big, and learn when to keep walking down the road beyond the game. Turn every gambling opportunity into a fun and profitable night of entertainment with the confidence that you are in control of the experience.

# Why Magick?

Gambling is a past-time long since rooted in human existence. An inexplicable tie between gambling and human nature has predominantly presented itself throughout the chronology of time. Equally intertwined with society is the pursuit of victory. As long as people have gambled, they have found ways to increase their luck. Historians unearthed Chinese tiles dating back to 2300 BC, suggesting they incorporated primitive lottery games into society for civic purposes. Sophocles' writings are the first Greek documentations of dice, and a discovery in an Egyptian tomb proved them older. Greek and Roman laws against dicing within city limits gave birth to gambling chips, and evidence suggests paper playing cards originated in 9th-century China as a possible primitive game of domino. Almost immediately, people became aware that gambling was a convenient mechanism to entertain the citizens and generate revenue for the social reformation of cities and governments. From the evolution of primitive Baccarat, Blackjack, and Roulette into the casino megalithic games they are today to the mobile slots and sports gaming apps people carry in their pockets, people have been playing and paying taxes associated with calculated risk games for eons. Unsurprisingly, they've been evolving their approach to increase their luck in gambling for just as long!

Players have evolved ways to improve their odds alongside the strategy implemented in their games. Methods of improving the odds are just as intertwined with human nature as gambling. People often refer to these methods as getting lucky. But "getting lucky" isn't always that easy. It can include an extensive ritual for bringing luck or be as simple as carrying a lucky charm. As evident from the ancient beginnings of gambling, the diversity of culture heavily influences the practice of getting lucky. Throughout the ages, races and ethnicities developed myriads of habits, quirks, objects, talismans, and energy-raising routines to enhance their gambling luck. They drew inspiration from both old-world rituals and folk magick. People created lasting superstitions and passed them down through generations to attract luck and wealth. We recognize many lucky charms, unlucky numbers, betting etiquette, and hot streaks but must learn their origins and magickal implications. Lore passed down through the generations can reveal many magickal tips and rituals practiced successfully by ancestors and inspire novel adaptations to integrate with the pre-established routine.

Expanding the odds to win is the goal in any game, and incorporating a magickal boost to increase those odds is not a new concept. Studying the lifestyle of budding civilizations, an evident bond exists between the people's deeply held ritualistic behaviors of the time and their belief in magick. Superstition, divine intervention, and magick were a part of everyday life. They explored the astral-physical realm through intricate rites, rituals, and experiments with numbers, letters, and resources of the earth available to them. All aspects of their life had special preparation, and gambling was no different. Antiquated writing on caves shows a purposeful attempt to cleanse a space from bad luck and evil spirits, and folk music compositions stress the importance of charging mojo bags when luck is lost.

No matter the prescribed method, the objective remains to keep and attract luck.

As gambling evolved, so did the tradition of conjuring luck. The institution of swaying the outcome of a game of chance through ritual and divine intervention rapidly evolved into mental contemplations following groundbreaking numerical and astrological discoveries. Engaging historical and empirical data suggests early gambling magick is influenced by the study of space, probability, and mathematics. Many notorious scholars and influential people of power studied the relationship between numbers and explored the potential scientific benefits of enacting magick in gambling. The relation of numbers was made evident through gaming. It inspired some mathematicians to create a correlation between numbers and magickal concepts, and numerology was born. Early Numerologists suggested a heavy connection between reasoning and reality. They proposed numbers and letters revealed patterns in nature, and people could influence their environment if they could decipher them. Numbers became connected to letters, then planets, animals, astrological signs, and even personalities. Evidence demonstrated there is a magickal key to conjuring luck, and that's not just hocus pocus.

Applicable numerology rapidly expanded the minds of the people. The suggestion that numbers could increase positive vibrations in the environment captivated the attention of scholars, oracles, religious figures, organizations, and laymen alike. Rooted in the beginnings of life in Mesopotamia, Sumerians used their understanding of numbers to initiate the infantile steps toward determining angles and time. At the same time, Egyptians bestowed powerful symbolic associations to numbers dedicated to divinity, prophecy, and energy. Pythagoras, an early mathematician who elaborated both concepts from there, combined his findings with the occult by assigning numbers to letters of the alphabet and explaining their vibrational frequencies. Number pattern developments in Middle Eastern cultures are often used to interpret religious texts and reveal hidden meanings to their believers. Entirely around the world, societies have found ways to promulgate the relationship between the natural and the supernatural by understanding how to harness and direct magickal energy for positive benefits.

Naturally, practicality is the mother of habit. The apparent advantages of adopting numerology for psychic cleansing and seeking divine guidance are overwhelming. Still, the versatility of including mystic rituals in business and entertainment also proved monetarily lucrative. The aristocracy and governments saw the potential to tax wealth gained through entertainment. The ignoble saw an opportunity to climb the social ladder by accumulating extra wealth, and both classes used magick to influence their luck to accomplish the goal. Transcending from ancient times into the 19th and the 20th-century, contemporaries such as Eliphas Levi, Gerard Encausse, L. Dow Balliett, Dr. Juno Jordan, and Cherio (William John Warner) maintained lifestyles by utilizing the systemic traditions of mingling occult magick with wealth, personality, and power. In the 21st century, social standing has become less critical than monetary wealth, and freedom from most bygone instabilities re-sparked an interest in gaining a gambling advantage. Still, the effort is notoriously regarded as selfishly profitable, and many discourage the practice. A litany of literary works exist as a precis to magickal gambling. Fewer works substantiate and justify the results of persistent measures to attract luck. Pushing the envelope to cover the gap, the need to collect the documented magick associated with attracting luck and wealth in a simple volume became objectively clear. Despite the pop-culture references, mainstream acceptance of glyphs and occult symbols, and widespread superstitions surrounding sports culture and betting becoming second nature, we are unconscious of the magickal potential that breathes on the fringe of our senses.

Becoming privy to the connection between conscious spiritual manipulation and results in the physical realm may kindle ethical questions regarding this avocation. Perceived interference with the natural law of the world is a sensitive subject. Proposing access to the power to control the flow of positive and negative energy can sound too good to be true for some and like blasphemy to others. Many disputes endure over the degree to which a person can influence their environment with magick. Proponents of limited magickal intervention in gambling cite abstract concepts of fate and destiny as logical pre-determined balances to the macrocosm. It is thought that skewing the universal balance forces an amelioration of the bias, and consequences vary for not adhering to natural law. Detractors of those assumptions operate on various idiosyncratic assertions themselves.

Generally speaking, copious amounts of ordinary folklore references provide a solid foundation for ethical counterarguments. Observing the mannerisms and lifestyles of humans over time, paying particular attention to their efforts to draw luck and wealth to themselves, it can be acknowledged that a natural balance doesn't necessarily require equal distribution of either luck or wealth. Many wealth and luck rituals are very mundane and don't require much preparation. Nor do they require asking for divine intervention in most cases. Folk magick, for example, primarily focuses on attracting more energy with less effort. If a magickal affix to an object or action waivers or begins to fail, it indicates that the previous magickal processes must be repeated. Through trial and error, many customs were derived to draw luck and positively infuse lucky charms. Applying a magickal touch to gambling endeavors can have excellent results and doesn't have to be a dog and pony show. Simple applications of standard household items have proven to pack a punch when conjuring a winning streak.

On the other hand, formal tone, invocation of deity, and sermons for formal rites vs. folk rites influence a significant portion of opinions on magickal ethics. Determining the efficacy of each ritual and how to interpret the results will depend on the foundation of the individual. Elaborate ceremonial and religious masses are as prevalent as simple instructions for candle magick and mojo bags. Still, depending on the rites performed, reactions tend to fluctuate regarding the aftermath of a magickal endeavor. A person's approach, follow through, and intent within their rituals will guide how they measure their results. This includes coming to conclusions based on the ideology and roots behind the magick.

Usually, a baseline influences every aspect of magickal workings. Hoodoo, Voodoo, some Folk Magick, and some Witchcraft sects are indifferent to acknowledging any repercussive karmic or scientific ramifications associated with working with magick for personal gain. Crafting a lucky charm bag, carrying a lucky object, wearing lucky colors, growing lucky plants, or cooking with lucky herbs hardly seems to pose an ethical dilemma to the average person. Instead, practitioners of magick who base their work on predominantly religious or karmic foundations emphatically emphasize the potential hazards of interfering with the natural balance. Prospecting the implications of pre-determined fate and destiny, closely tied to an individual's beliefs, drawing luck and prosperity that one doesn't already possess can wreak havoc instead of being beneficial in the long run. Therefore, individuals engaging in the employment of magick for luck in gambling should consider all the factors that could influence the outcome of their desires.

Opposite the ethical quandaries is a discussion over intent and inevitable outcome. Being bound to physical limitations, natural law will always play a factor in magickal workings, and tangible results will always account for measurable success. Enumerable benefits will vary from actor to actor, and any factors, such as internal or external turmoil, vibrational frequencies in the environment, or harmful intent, can influence the magickal product. All that suggests is the crafting of magickal gambling spells and charms will need to be honed, adjusted periodically, and monitored. Consistent paradigms must emerge to aid the furtherance of justifying the use of magickal luck in gambling, and differing archetypes with overlapping congruous results while remaining parallel must be recognized. Fruitful endeavors of drawing fortune and profit are achieved through infinite combinations of materials and rituals. The proof of this fact is evident through the lasting superstitions of the ages and the prosperity acquired from the calculations of those who believe. Our predecessors left behind extraordinary information available to anyone ready to ignite their own fortune, but that's not all. They also left the literal building blocks of the same influential energy they discovered.

After the metaphysical forces are summoned and have satisfied their intended goals, many rites will encourage returning the power to the ether and reviewing the appropriate steps to recall them. Magickal items will gradually lose energy over time, and carrying around a supercharged magickal item or resonating on a higher frequency for an extended period drags on a person's cosmic energy. In science, we are reminded that energy in motion tends to stay in motion, and energy spent must be replenished. Therefore, a need arises to restock the magickal atmosphere. Lending some extra credibility to the idea of a semblance of universal balance, riding a hot streak must come to an end. Properly preparing for and adapting to shifts in the energy fields can take time to find blueprints for mastering. The practice of dispersing that energy is as specific as the method of raising it. Even the simple chore of storing a magickal item or the ritual of forgoing the washing of lucky fabrics are variances of grounding exercises. Energy stored in magickal items will leech slowly when the items are not actively utilized. On the contrary, items that are active more than not can expel their power at an accelerated rate. In both circumstances, the energy returns to the environment to be recycled later.

Aside from directly returning the energy to the ether, it is essential to allow magickally charged items time to release energy at a deceleration rate when the item is not actively implemented. This procedure will affect the frequency and potency of the item's performance. The concept is noteworthy as venting extra vibrational energy is beneficial and satisfying for an individual and replenishes the astral plane. Over time, a talisman or rite that conjures luck successfully will need a recharge or recast to remain effective, and, in theory, releasing unspent energy will recycle it to be used again. Conditioning the senses to synchronize with the existing forces in the surroundings allows stagnant energy to flow more freely. Free-flowing positive and negative energy can be more easily drawn from the environment and still interact independently from directed or collected forces. The magickal plane operates like a psychic pipeline transmitting frequencies back and forth in the atmosphere. Manifested energy is spent on the same plane it is called from. The natural tendency of energy is to return to the pot. Implementing a solid plan for grounding residual energy and storing charms and other lucky items to achieve maximum results when conjuring luck for gambling ensures there will be energy to draw from later.

In conjunction with closing the psychic tap, another often over-sighted topic to talk about is when to abstain from betting. Where magick is a potent tool intended to boost the luck of an individual in addition to strategy and numerical contemplation, it can not be abused as a crutch or used as an excuse for a gambling addiction. Positive, productive magick, for luck or otherwise, is best practiced with a healthy mindset. Regardless of the techniques and methods proven to aid in gaining luck and wealth, they are not quick fixes or get-rich-quick schemes. Magick should not be expected to bring about fantastical results overnight. Flagrant and fickle dabbling with energy and magick leads to adverse outcomes. Making poor choices on top of that can lead to worse. Recorded results make a difference when the adverse effects outweigh the positive ones. Establishing a pattern allows for early detection of when to re-evaluate a losing strategy. This re-stresses the importance of keeping meticulous archives of past performance. Recognizing when luck is no longer in the energy field is the most mighty magickal ability to possess. It will help to identify the right time to walk away from the table. Waning energy that is influencing an individual coming off a hot streak, especially without their knowledge, can cause an addictive response. Know when to hold the bets, especially when the odds turn.

Tips, charms, chants, solid mathematical logic, and all the divine powers in the universe are not substitutes for maintaining control of a gambling wager. People can find the ability to influence their luck intoxicating and lose control of their rational thinking. Keep in mind the energy conjured is a metaphysical force of nature. An otherwise sensible individual can have their judgment clouded by the increased energy field. As the stakes are raised and the odds of winning decrease, the desire to turn the luck can outweigh the unsustainable losses. However, allowing the impulse to dominate the situation will negate all preparation strategies entirely. Winning without ever losing is statistically and realistically unfathomable. Set appropriate expectations of results alongside a gambling strategy that includes a hard line to walk away from the table. Money at risk should never be money that can't be lost comfortably. An experienced gambler understands this is as much a part of the game as all the topics covered thus far.

Overall, as gambling became more prominent throughout the evolution of time, so did the effects of the highs and lows of superstitious gamblers. Archaic proverbs, religious doctrine, and even modern fictional characters cryptically forewarn of emotional burdens surrounding the ebb and flow of good luck and wealth. Parables abound recounting mass wealth accumulation and the rise of a person's popularity while being associated with occult workings that end in destitution and woe. The tales are as old as time. As a result, the need for a comprehensive and concise manual to attract luck and wealth while gambling became clear. This book's objective will be to accumulate a body of work that legitimizes the tradition of using occult magick in gambling while simultaneously exhibiting illustrations of notorious individuals known to engage and further the advancement of folk magick and vibration theory. This guide will be essential to incorporating magick into many gambling strategies as efficiently as possible. No one has hours to waste on researching proven, efficient resources for impactful results. This compressed edition of historical references, cataloged scientific and mathematical theories, and familiar Folklore and Witchcraft rituals will inspire a multitude of gamblers to adopt a new strategy to attract luck and wealth. The secrets passed down through the generations can illuminate a winning atmosphere. Draw from any combination of the corroborated demonstrations of effective magickal gambling strategies and comprehend why they work. Base a strategy on occult magick rooted in tradition. Boost any level of play with a natural and logical approach to gambling with a magickal edge.

# History of Magick

At first glance, gambling magick sounds like New Age spiritual mumbo jumbo because a majority of the history surrounding this art is shrouded by conflicting religious opinions and lost records in time. Linear connections between magick and gambling have been hidden and misconstrued equally, but an overarching examination of the knowledge accumulated throughout history reveals how surprisingly deep the belief in the arcane arts really is. Some of the oldest games of wealth and luck are intertwined with seeking divine guidance and basic probability. Whether drawing from the ancient Egyptians, medieval English, or contemporary essayists, today's gamblers have plenty of historical justification for exploring their opportunity to attract luck and wealth with magick. Correlations dating back to the glyphs of early civilizations carved into cave walls strongly suggest and verify that humans have always acknowledged supernatural forces around them. Each region of the world has a dynamic archive of naming and identifying astral implications and interpreting mystic energies. Many, if not all, aspects of life in the past incorporated a spiritual connection to unseen vibrations in the atmosphere. Artifacts bearing long-forgotten texts, symbols that have lost meanings, and depictions of ceremonies no longer practiced provide context to the intentions and outcomes of magick in their lives. Despite most discoveries having a popular religious connotation, a hefty dose of the catalog contains a firm belief in vibrational energy, mathematical probability and outcome, and simple magick.

Most people assume gaming and gambling origins are spawned only from the need to satisfy entertainment desires, but early records have proven that the invention of dice and ancient scripts on game boards and other items are founded in spiritual divination. The discovery of the Egyptian twenty-sided die etched with depictions of a known God of the era on each face alludes to their primary purpose being to seek divine guidance or advice, not entertainment. Knucklebone dice, one of the earliest discovered, are thought to have been utilized for 'yes' or 'no' questions, and the preceding two-sided throwing sticks suggest they had similar primitive use. Even the oldest recognized board game, Senet, a rudimentary Egyptian version of the game Backgammon, appeared to have the game's objective to be a transformation into the afterlife. Over time, the game board appeared in many drawings and accounted as rare artifacts recovered through unearthing tomb remains and pyramid decor. It is now seen as the "original game of death," as more recent paintings show players playing against an invisible opponent. A rendition of the game on the tomb walls of Hesy-Re exists as the oldest known reference to Senet. Progressing through the decades, the game mutated into an early Ouija board and became notorious for communicating with the dead. People continued to exhibit repeated efforts to gain deeper introspection into becoming wealthy, lucky, and endowed by their creators. Therefore, integrating their religion and superstition without leaving behind an instruction manual has led to wild speculation and intense debate surrounding the matter of intent. For this body of work, a case for the co-existence of astral factors under the purposeful intent of sentient individuals to attract luck in gambling will be based on the results of past performers of arcane arts, occult magick, and folk magick. Examples of religious ceremonies and deity beseechment may be referenced. No example should be misconstrued as an endorsement for or indictment of any religion, creed, belief, tradition, or sect. All manners of magickal workings will be sovereign to the individual practitioner.

The messy entanglement of gambling and religion is thick. Parallel to magickal operations, seeking divine intervention from a named deity or higher power is a shared experience in most people's lives in one way or another. Therefore, having the faith that a godly force will also cushion the outcome of a gambling endeavor is not uncommon. Multi-deity pantheons assembled by humans around the world harbor gods and goddesses associated with luck, prosperity, and wealth. Civilizations built their societies around appeasing these entities with the expectation that they would be blessed and bountiful by doing so. Evidenced by the evolution of the Egyptian Senet game from entertainment value to telephone to the dead, sheer enjoyment wasn't enough emotional satisfaction for early contests to become popularized on their own. Gaming and eventually gambling adopted a profound bond to the religiosity of a particular region in any given era. The exploration of the kaleidoscope of the ethnic and multicultural roots of gambling showcases a connection of the people to a multi-faceted belief in extenuating forces influencing outcomes in the universe. Denominations and applications contrast drastically, yet the overall results repeat consistently. A desire to explore the potential to psychologically manipulate the outcome of a wager became an exciting opportunity for all classes of citizens to explore. It began to inject new ideas for creating games and permitting gambling to bolster social and governmental institutions. A practice that quickly caught fire and rapidly spread.

Early archives reveal the first crude lottery system initiated for the ruling government's monetary fundraising beginning under the Chinese Han Dynasty. This system is believed to have funded the Great Wall of China. Primeval keno-style slip discs were issued to citizens with the assurance that they would be compensated with a valuable reward from the emperor. The sentiment of the time was that emperors, kings, and other rulers were of divine right or, in other words, chosen by the Gods. This would influence the citizens to buy into the governmentally approved gambling of the time. In loose theory, they would be rewarded for participating by the divine entities that blessed the rulers. This overlapping of religious undertones and divine intervention can be the source of misconceptions surrounding the religious and magickal dynamics of gambling. It can create much confusion if the focus is too close to the subject. Instead, analyzing trends over a broad storyline of effective strategies to generate luck and prosperity lends much more compelling evidence to consider when incorporating magick in gambling.

Games were often given metaphorical and symbolic associations with real-life risks and rewards after creation in Greek and Roman culture. The communities of the time were flush with artistic and philosophical citizens who dabbled as much in abstract contemplation as they did in filling political positions of power. Origins of the Game of Alea are steeped in both. Credited to Palamedes, a Euboean prince in Greek mythology, the game was allegedly invented during the Trojan War. It pits two players against each other, rolling lead dice to move pawns across the board. Rolls and moves are based on the probability of the outcome of the dice.

The throwing of random objects as dice allowed for multi-purpose effects and strategies. Depending upon the complexity of the object's shape, the physical space in which they are tossed, how it is pitched, and how it lands will determine how to wield the hands prior to releasing the throw. These small hand gestures greatly influence the odds of the dice. The number of spaces to travel on the game board and the area of the landing space for the dice affect the probability of the game. Both strategies can be implemented alone or simultaneously and may be easily adapted by all classes of citizens. Techniques such as shaking the hands, snapping the wrists, banking the dice, or landing them flat became observable actions that made a difference in the outcome of the game.

On the other hand, studying the probability of outcomes in number relations in dice games became an even more advanced strategy. The affinity of each class to be drawn to a particular method of playing could be explained through the metaphorical implications of the names of the games. Evocative titles such as latrunculi, which translates to 'little robbers,' reges, or 'kings,' duodecim scripta (Twelve Writings), and Alea reinforced the conventionalized opinions surrounding the intelligence level of the players of certain games. Connotations associated with the stereotyping names of the contests are some of the last pieces remaining to complete the puzzle of their original instructions and rules. The games were also a good indication of a person's social status. Both gambling and gaming have always been a vice and a virtue. In the most benign interpretations, the invention served as a mere distraction to pass the time. Upon further scrutiny, understanding the medley of money, political power, and cosmic influence in gambling can enlighten modern gamblers about the powerful effects of these primitive competitions.

As previously mentioned, dicing and gambling were illegal within some city limits, yet enforcing those bans was seldom carried out. This was due to the fact that many politicians, emperors, kings, rulers, oracles, priests, and scholars were gamblers of the day. Playwrights, authors, and poets penned the last remnants of literature that preserve the references to gambling of the era, and as the culture advanced, so did the competition. Matches once thought up to while away the hours were made much more intense by adding some risk and reward, and soon everyone was partaking in an equal opportunity to stretch their luck. This all led to many people on every level honing their skills to maximize the profitability of the gamble. Therefore, in addition to positive intellectual advancements in mathematics and science, it also helped to create a sub-genre of mundane magickal tips, tricks, and charms.

Unfortunately, it also had negative impacts on society. From notable nobles to insignificant inhabitants, the high of winning it all could overwhelm individuals to their demise. Although to stress the fact that religious persecution did not actually fuel the legal enforcement of gambling bans despite popular belief, historical scholars note that a gambler who lost everything was often mocked and ridiculed. Then, being displaced in power and reduced to poverty, possibly to debts, a legal procedure could later result. The upper classes of society were also more sophisticated than their secondary citizens. They often considered the lower-class gaming strategy too reminiscent of hogs and considered their methods below them. The hierarchy of the people is crucial for context to frame a modern opinion on using magick in gambling. The two independent courses of basic magick and ritual magick can be explained and elaborated upon by this split in social configuration. This period of gaming evolution became a pinnacle for gambling. Rapid connections between movement and mathematical reasoning were becoming popular while contemporaneously enhancing a humble, pragmatic approach to gambling. Regardless of status, anyone could invent a lucky strategy.

A manuscript of the period scribed by historian Ou-yang Hsiu dates 'sheet dice' back to the mid-Tang Dynasty era. The initial prints described were made on silk and bamboo scraps, but the invention of parchment paper was often thought to have resulted from the desire to make tiles out of lighter material that would be easier to inscribe. Games and gambling ideas weren't the only thing flourishing at this time. Spiritual and religious growth, in addition to monetary advancements such as paper currency, were also maturing. All aspects of society fed off one another. The foundation for expanding a gambling game repertoire was just beginning to set and dry when the Kuei T'ien Lu, a collection of anecdotes from the eleventh century, appeared. It was the beginning of religious warnings against repugnant behaviors. The Chinese used paper domino-style and picture cards for entertainment, forms of divinity, and drawing luck, but they expanded paper printing for money and religious texts. The bifurcation of printing cards on either paper or other materials, such as ivory or bone, appeared briefly in production. This inspired the MaJong-style tiles, but the harder organic matter proved challenging to illustrate, and paper became king. In fact, as the ability to manufacture paper and printing press technology broke free from Chinese monopoly, the Arabic, Dutch, English, French, German, Italian, and Spanish adopted a similar path of progressing their own adaptation of cards, texts, and banknotes. Coins and cash are apparent examples of ancient history that survived until the modern age. Lesser prominent examples reflect on more profound implications of yore.

In the late thirteenth century, Marco Polo sailed as a Venetian explorer and returned to Italy after scouring and voyaging the Silk Road in Asia. He brought a new method of stamping intricate sketches onto parchment paper and tiles that he learned on his journey. Paper production eventually dominated the printing practice, and through this procedure, the initial creation of the first set of playing cards, The Devil's Picture Books, was born. Evidently, the ambiguous naming trends continued cross-country, which helped fuel religious restrictions on gaming and gambling cards. Arabic doctrine, in particular, originating from the Middle Eastern nations, has a guideline outlying religious duties to God called the Tratado de Hispa. It expresses how indulgence in gambling or gaming can lead to uncivil behavior, violence, or idleness. An indoctrination of religious undertones and superstition began to bubble under the skin of the newly formed technologies of the era.

Diffusion occurred comprehensively at the time in all areas of business, leisure, science, and spirituality. As such, playing cards dispersed throughout the masses in every empire, and the accelerated emulation of the games resulted in innumerable appellations. Frequently, these cognomens overlapped one another, and games were overwhelmingly popular outside of their originating countries. For example, Tarrochi is a game invented by the Italian man Felix Falguiere, who is also credited with deriving the modern model of Baccarat, a game previously accredited to the French. The Devil's Picture Book morphed into the first tarot deck, leading to Tarrochi, which became the crux of Baccarat en Banco, Chemin de Fer, Le Her, and Macao. These games trace further down the line to Vignt-et-un, a French title meaning twenty-one, and the roots of modern BlackJack. In Spain, they were playing Ventiuna (21), Trente-un (31), or Quinze (15), all being precursors to our modern casino gaming selections.

The Darwinistic nature of gambling adaptation over generations is fascinating and inspiring. Development of the Roulette Wheel, dice towers, poker chips, hand signals, and game terminology is cloaked in perpetual mysticism. As more complex match rule sets were made, numerical combinations and patterns emerged. In turn, the people's strategy to comprehend the patterns became more entwined with religious and practical superstitions. Their mannerisms, habits, and aversions dictated the type of games they played and how they played them, including eventually implementing ingenious ways to increase House Odds and establish the House Rules we are familiar with today. Moving the progress ever forward. Today, slot machines, mobile poker apps, DraftKings-style sports betting websites, and many other technology-based gambling opportunities operate by generating or observing randomized outcomes to determine contest winners. These factors cause deviations in gaming strategies opposite to table-based card game strategies involving multiple players. By revamping the forgotten history of gaming, old strategy can prove worthy of prolonging and expounding.

# Methods of Magick

It is common practice to habitually engage in many superstitious behaviors and not even realize it. A considerable amount of religious observances can be regarded as superstitious engagements. The word itself is defined as a trusting belief in magick, chance, or a false conception of causation; a notion maintained despite evidence to the contrary; or an irrational abjection of God or the supernatural by the Merriam-Webster dictionary. Plenty of opposing religious groups regard traditions or idols outside their canon as sacrilegious, and volumes of theological texts and rituals account for diverse superstitions. As well as the numbers that are associated with Gods and Goddesses expanded in numerology. Still, folk tales recounted to elucidate enigmatic natural occurrences and salient behaviors that yield reoccurring consequences are also prominent sources of superstitious behavior. Although this book may refer back to the religious origins, the general focus under our scope will be successful strategies of magickal influence. Specifically, Numerology, Folk Magick, and various forms of HooDoo, VooDoo, and Witchcraft will be discussed at length. Using the historical framework and premise set up in the previous chapter, the remainder of this section will elaborate on techniques and lucky gambling methods. The definition of the word superstition will be used in the context of the dictionary meaning for the purposes of this book. Therefore, a case will be laid for the value of recording an illustrated path of consistent outcomes to practicing successful magick, not just rehearsing a superstition.

Our starting point will be a widely familiar one. Lucky charms. Lucky charms are seemingly ordinary objects infused with the ability to bring the owner or possessor increased favorable likelihoods. Charms run the gamut from being extremely notable to wildly obscure. A preponderance of society is well aware of the roots of the four-leaf clover and the general shine of having a lucky horseshoe, but far less can explain precisely how or where the luck comes from. Why is this significant? The answer is for accuracy, of course. Learning the collage of reasoning behind how lucky charms became considered lucky can make them easier to replicate. The clover, for example, is a great starting piece. Leaves of the typical three-leaf clover are famous in common lore. In the Middle Ages, children spread tales that carrying a four-leaf clover allowed for the ability to see fairies. In Celtic Druidry, they were carried to see evil spirits. The four-leaf clovers were special because they were uncommon, which is precisely what made them lucky. Typical three-leaf clovers had a virtue assigned to each leaf grown. One for love, one for faith, and one for hope. The fourth leaf that grew was considered lucky and, therefore, was associated with luck. Still, the rarity of the four-leaf clover goes deeper. In fact, the genetic anomaly only occurs once for every 5,076 three-leaf clovers grown. With this extra information, it is safe to conclude reproducing a lucky clover is highly unlikely, but it is fortunate to find one. The lucky horseshoe, on the other hand, makes for an excellent pivot point.

Stemming from the same Celtic folklore, horseshoes and their stories date back to the Stone Age. As nomads migrated into Northern Europe and the British Isles carrying clovers for the ability to see the unseen, they also thought of a way to prevent those undesirable entities from entering their dwellings. Thus, hanging a horseshoe at the front door was invented. The idea was to hang a horseshoe on display outside the residence, open end up to resemble the crescent crown of the Celtic Moon God, and that would spook away the evil or mischievous spirits. Over time, this observance misplaced its original intent. Alternative lore was bestowed upon the horseshoe. Positioning up for catching luck and position down for dropping luck into the home became the new purpose of hanging a horseshoe at the front entrance. The more popular secular explanations became the enduring rituals for harnessing luck in both the case of the horseshoe and the clover. As the intent changed, so did the method to attract luck. These widespread specimens exemplify the capability of seemingly ordinary objects or plants to draw luck and perfectly illustrate how easy it is to alter methods to suit varying goals.

Countless charms people would be most acquainted with are redundant and mass-produced. Rabbit feet, fuzzy dice, precious metal coins or scraps, jewelry, gems, religious icons or idols, and many other trinkets are harbored as lucky charms and believed to be a factor in a gambling endeavor. Their popularity is undoubtedly enough to keep them relevant, but they have also brought luck and fortune to the small businesses that sell them. Gambling revenue hit records in both 2021 and 2022. Although lucky charms (outside of the breakfast cereal) are not a specifically identifiable metric on the stock market, the success of magickal amulets is evident from their accepted presence in the gambling world, and judging by gambling sales, that's a massive number of individuals who potentially buy into lucky charms. The more people who utilize these tchotchkes, the more eclectic their methods of attracting luck. For example, a piece of jewelry could be extra lucky on a specific day of the week or on a particular body part, or carrying the last coin from a winning pot could extend the winning streak to the next wager. Simply because a token is overly commercialized or sold for profit doesn't render it useless for magickal intentions. There are ample ways to infuse these common artifacts with profitability.

Moving from the acquainted into the more esoteric curiosa but expounding upon anthologizing magickal infusion, the next topic will be Mojo bags. Mojo bags are commonly associated with African-American Hoodoo, but the activity of collecting magickal ingredients to create a powerful amulet crossed through Voodoo, Witchcraft, and Folk Magick as well. Typical Mojo bags start with a drawstring bag, traditionally made of flannel but can vary per manner of preference or intent, then get filled meticulously with commodities tailored to the desired magickal charge. Standard fillers include dirt, herbs, inscribed wax or wood pieces, semi-precious stones or rocks, ivory, bone, earth elements, or any other combination of magickal concoctions. The flexibility of the Mojo bag is what makes it an excellent, utterly versatile magick charm for luck. Ingredients for a mojo bag can be symbolically deep, or they can be an analogy for the intent, or they can simply be filled with notable lucky items. For example, precious stones formed by rare occurrences in nature or evolution are powerful energy generators due to their unique composition, and wood and wax objects can be used to inscribe glyphs and symbols to incorporate into the bags. The more intricate the intent is entwined with the contents of the Mojo bag, the more potent the amulet will become. This option for diversity and customization in attracting luck became fundamental to emancipating Mojo bags in all cultures and creating a brand-new taxonomy of magick.

Medicine bags, prayer bags, trick bags, Tobies, Lucky Hands, and Gris-gris are all aliases of the Mojo bag. To unearth the bag's roots, start with the etymology of the word Mojo. Originating from the Kongo language, Mojo derives from the word 'mooyo'. Mooyo refers to "spirits that dwelt within magickal charms" and a cavity for storing a magickal item known as nkisi. Gris-gris is another literal translation of Mojo, adopted in Louisiana from Mande, another West African language. Mojos and Gris-gris were passed down from the first Muslim ethnic groups imported from Sierra Leone into the Americas through the trans-Atlantic slave trade. They taught the crafting of the satchels to African-American slaves, who then began to incorporate their own Christian and Islamic religiosity into the pouches. Native American Indians, on the other hand, had been crafting their own medicine bags for centuries before the idea transited from abroad. Pop-culture references of the twenty-first century redefine Mojo as meaning virility and sexuality. Still, the concept is gathering a collection of items to achieve a desired outcome. The bag is carefully constructed, tied, and blessed, then worn, hung, displayed, or hidden for the designer's intended purpose. This method became wildly popular because of the ease of the ritual.

It inspired adaptation and growth in potions and spell work as a popular tradition growing across cultures.

Spell-work and potions may sound conceptual and arcane, but any misconceptions can be cleared up if education is diffused and knowledge is preserved. A quick glance at history thus far has demonstrated multiple correlations between humans and the environment. Examining this connection, the relationship between plants and intent became apparently beneficial. Hence, mixing potions and writing spell-work was born.

Spell-work and potions may sound abstract and arcane, but any misconceptions can be cleared up if education is diffused and knowledge is preserved. A quick glance at history thus far has demonstrated multiple correlations between humans and the environment. Examining this connection, the relationship between plants and intent became apparently beneficial. Hence, mixing elixirs and writing spell-work was born. Hunting and gathering at inception were survival techniques, but when humanity started to build civilizations, they began to advance their understanding of relationships between resources. Modern herbology, Botany, and additional contemporary medicines we use in hospitals today have deeply seeded roots in early potion-making. A present-day garden at Mount Grace Priory still grows plants 15th-century monks would have grown for primitive medicines or potions and educates the public on how they influenced scientific progress. Continuing the trend of intermingling religion and the mystic. The practice of potion mixing and spell-work resembles the early formation of the scientific method. An intention would be framed, and the manner of action to perpetrate the desired outcome would begin. This would include utilizing any chants, hand gestures, ingredients, tools, or spells known to be empirical for the outcome. Spells and rituals often describe the list of materials and their purpose while being added during the production of a tincture. Rites and religious ceremonies use heavy symbolism in their prayers while preparing sacraments. In both examples, spell-work and potion-making go hand in hand.

Potion-making and spell-working seem removed from Mojo bags, but the premise is basically the same, especially for luck. Many of the same herbs and plants that get sealed into Mojo bags can alternatively be used in potions and spell-work. The elemental compositions of the plants were eventually found to have beneficial effects when ingested and applied to the skin, in addition to having the positive energy they exhibit in Mojo bags. The versatility of plants and simple substitutions of spell-work to tailor intent enables the practice of potion-making to flourish beyond mere luck. Digesting the concoctions and absorbing effects via the skin proffered more concrete physical outcomes. A vial could be mixed to calm the nerves, sharpen the mind, or render your adversary out of sorts. The options were restricted only to the conscience of the individual. But the art of potion-making is more comprehensive than all herbs and no substance. It encompasses cooking and processing food, too. Chinese culture serves fish for luck, and in Spain, eating twelve grapes at midnight on New Year's Eve brings luck for each month of the year. Entire meals are cooked for the sole purpose of bringing wealth and fortune to the diner.

In contrary fashion, as previously discussed, some sects of religious followings, witches, and cultures may strongly prohibit any personal gain involving these approaches to magick. Some glyphs, Gods, icons, symbols, and spells may be offensive to some people when used to invoke monetary gain. This can severely impact the results of a magickal potion or spell. Individuals themselves influence the energy in addition to the ingredients they use in their spell-work. Accordingly, if the person attempting to cast the spell or interact with the elements has an internal conflict with any components, they will experience unsuccessful results. Color coordinations, numerical associations, texts, and other emphatic symbolisms only have the energy a person bestows into them through their beliefs. The ultimate element in magick is the psychic bond between the practitioner and the craft. The inability of so many to be in tune with frequencies in their environments or cater to the energy they raise by bringing magickal items into their aura can lead to unprofitable results. The unseen factor of emotional commitment should be considered when picking a strategy to draw fortune and wealth. Which was the mission of 21st-century contemporaries.

As the common folk experimented with easily accessible magickal talismans, the higher-educated citizens expanded their mental contemplations. Mathematics and science grew seamlessly alongside Folk magick, tarot, and ceremonial magick and contributed to it immensely. The ancient Greek philosopher Pythagoras, who dabbled in many political and philosophical activities, was the first to construct a theory that all things in existence could be expressed in numbers. He was the father of earth-shattering mathematical theories and the man to discover Venus. His initial findings in math and science gave way to modern scholars, astrologers, numerologists, chiromancy, and clairvoyants. Using the premise of his theories, volumes were produced in droves to expound on vibrational energy and how it could be used for profit and gain. That, in turn, made the authors themselves famously successful.

# Numerology, Planetary Alignment and Vibrations

Recalling the previous methodology encountered thus far, plenty of trinkets, brews, and prayers can be employed to attract luck and wealth. Many of those results were intended consequences, and others occurred naturally. Some magickal commodities can accumulate energy through formation, growth, or evolution; those articles can be implemented together for potency. Or, they can be focused and used singularly as well. But what if the psychic plane in which those talismans are made was also strategically manipulated? Could it be? Intellectuals and philosophers over the ages began to study the answers to those questions they found within numbers, letters, and planetary alignments. An urge to juxtapose humans with the universe and the divine became attractive to people looking to control the outcome of their desires. The dose of ingredients required to complete a task and the observable atmosphere of a practitioner's workspace reignited a relationship between numbers and psychic energy. Priests, theologists, oracles, and other clergymen were the first pioneers to associate early mathematics and religious thought. This was the infancy phase of numerology. Pythagoras, Plato, St. Augustine of Hippo, Eliphas Levi, and many others taught their personal ideology alongside their interpretation of early numerology. The mathematical adaptations, on the other hand, brought angles, time, space, and planetary magnetism into the conscious perspective of the people to evaluate physical causes and effects. Religious and practical explanations of the energy vibrations associated with the numbers were branching apart. One side of the divergence was spiritually linked, and the other was physical reality. Both sides could invariably demonstrate efficacy while being independent of each other, or they could also be used in concurrency. The only consistency to the logical theories was the consequences emanating from the numbers and the planetary alignments.

The Chaldean people, Pythagoras, and the Sumerians may have been the first to recognize a relationship between numbers and the astral plane, as astrology has also been observed since the dawn of time. However, notable contemporaries in the 19th, 20th, and 21st centuries have taken those initial findings and run with them. St. Augustine of Hippo, a Berber theologian, once wrote, " Numbers are the universal language offered by the deity to humans as confirmation of truth.". Thus, many people were fascinated by the idea of accessing a path to prosperity and began experimenting with numbers, letters, and the positioning of the heavens. They viewed this power as an ability to communicate with the divine. Oracles, scholars, religious figures, and politicians prone to speaking publicly began to perpetuate the notions of celestial power in math and science. Prominently, Dorotheus of Gaza and Eliphas Levi practiced and taught prophetic numerology as a way to receive direction from God and understand more profound meanings of the world. Their ideas were adopted by considerable groups of people to the extent that many religions banned the practice entirely by 325 A.D. This resulted in a more segregated separation that caused much of the education concerning the subject matter to have conflicting meanings and even mislead people depending on source material vs personal religious affiliations or beliefs. Instead of dying out, however, those interested in the occult proudly claimed the abstract practice and learned new ways to reincorporate the otherwise hidden meanings into accepted societal values.

Starting within the very roots of the word numerology, there is power. Before the updated terminology we are discussing was used, the practice was called arithmancy, derived from 'arithmos manteia,' meaning number divination. References to numerology weren't documented in historical archives until circa 1907. Various approaches exist to illustrate and define a system that expresses the vibrational frequencies of and assigns numerical values to letters. Still, the two most popular ones are the Chaldean and Pythagoras systems. The citizens were especially interested in the truths the systems could reveal. They expounded upon the foundation of both systems across the board, but early arithmancy focused mainly on divination. Over time, the more the magickal numbers were validated, the more popular they became. Mainly because they were associated with the word or guidance of the gods. But, the more widespread the technique became, the more benefits were acquired with the details they divulged. People tapping into the energy infused in their personalities exponentially. Writers, intellectuals, and clairvoyants were taking notice of the versatility of the number energy theory and began to teach and pen works expressing their ideas for additional implementations of the craft.

Sophisticated and religious citizens weren't the only people who benefitted from understanding and capitalizing on positive numerical vibrations. Numerology offered all levels of the citizenry a guide to explaining the reverberating atmosphere of the universe. Laymen, carpenters, farmers, and sometimes even unscrupulous community members were also interested in having a prosperous advantage. As previously mentioned, an individual's conscience is the only limitation to their intent. Practicing numerology and astrology became an accurate way to identify what a person's conscience might allow and what might make a person more successful in life. Then, these discovered revelations could be used for good or corrupt desires. But, a more widespread use of numerology is for attracting, discovering, and continuing luck. As more people observed their environment and implemented these magickal numbers, the repetitious conclusions that appeared began to build an entire dictionary of secret meanings and obscure luck. The more the system saw success, the faster and larger it grew.

The desire of the people to learn numerology was overwhelming and quickly met by advantageous individuals eager to teach the subject. Notable authors such as Dr. Juno Jordan, L. Dow Balliett, and Cheiro (William John Warner) found tremendously accurate results with lucky numbers, love attraction, fortune telling, and wealth accumulation. These writers could understand the number vibration theory so well they augmented the usefulness of the systems. Cheiro developed chiromancy or palm reading throughout his career, expanding on numerology. He impressed many famous figures in history, such as Mark Twain, Thomas Edison, and Grover Cleveland, with his accurate readings. Dow wrote an extensive library of books that explain number vibration theory, numerical philosophy, tone, and colors. She is regarded as the mother of numerology. Juno's work focused predominantly on love affiliations, but her probes into number personality vibration theory can prove to be vital information for numerology endeavors. The authors also looked to the heavens and observed the planets during their studies. They were beginning to realize the entire universe had a role in influencing cosmic vibrations. To validate their hypothesis' and ensure accurate results when an experiment was reproduced, they began documenting and reporting their findings to others.

Learning from the expanded ideas and applying the same techniques of mingling tactics to construct spells, Mojo bags, rituals, and potions, numerology can be applied over and into any strategy of magick. The day of the week or alignment of the planets is just as imperative to a successful magickal outcome as mixing the right combination of herbs. Numbers portray intricate patterns of nature and create concrete effects in the physical realm. The description of the values of numbers and letters shined true to a vast population. This made the luck-drawing numerical sequences and the vibrations associated with them the most favorable among the people. Individuals then began to study the potential of interwoven destiny that their birth dates tied to their personal traits and characteristics. This included early astrological associations and planetary alignments at the time of birth. These elaborate calculations and cumulation of intimately personalized numbers accurately corresponded with astral arrangements and constructed solid profiles of individuals. Then, once armed with information sensitive to a specific person, a lucky action, number, or other magickal remedy can be assembled.

Similarly to the idea in numerology of assigning value to letters and exploring those relationships, astrology assigned importance to stars and constellations. Astrology expanded on number theory and angles, contributed to the depth of personality charts, and assisted in individualizing productive methods of attracting luck or fortune. Planets were observed to have powerful effects on humanity due to their stationing in the solar system. Planetary positioning in the sky, their size, and sometimes their illumination dictated their ruling forces and how they affected inhabitants on Earth. Navigators, farmers, religious factions, and philosophers have used planetary power for many practical purposes since recorded history began. However, using astrology for divination and psychic manipulation was often viewed as a pseudoscience. Despite the fact many priests, rulers, and medicine men wrote extensively about the correlations they found in the heavens, due to evolving religious doctrine and conflicting connotations assigned to the material, astrology was cast aside by the masses save a select few. Individuals compelled to explore the potential of planetary power soon became the outcasts of society. The science of calculating and accounting for psychic energy was a formidable assertion to explain. Still, the evidence was undeniable.

People are unable to escape the obvious effects of the planet around them. They feel the warmth of the sun, the chill of a breeze, and the dirt on their hands. They understand how each element is somehow tied to planetary movement, yet the concept of unseen energy playing a role in their every activity seems far-fetched. However, that didn't stop many astrologers, occultists, numerologists, and commoners from developing alternative uses for astrology and numerology to prove the power existed. One of the subjects that got the most attention to prove the point was the art of attracting luck and wealth. Gambling became the perfect lure to entice an otherwise skeptical individual into dabbling in numerology, astrology, and magickal vibrations. Citizens who might otherwise be doubtful of or fear repercussions from pursuing this mystic force of nature gave an exception for strategy in gaming as it was seen as sheer entertainment and not particularly serious in any way.

Gambling methods were advancing from the late 1700s into and throughout the late 1800s, and the games themselves were metamorphosing. Roulette, poker, and slot machines were making waves as the hottest casino games on the market, becoming showcases in Monte Carlo and Paris. Variations of these games had been played for centuries, but the versions that emerged in the 19th century are much more familiar to today's modern gambler. Newer rule sets had an enriched emphasis on numbers, suits, colors, and combinations. The competitions became even more thrilling as the progressive pastimes incorporated random probability with mental skill to win large pots. The entire industry became a spectacle for players and spectators alike. The atmosphere of a crowd forming around the games added energy and a sense of critique from the crowd. Every bet was for all to see, as was every win and every loss. The aura of that pressure undoubtedly would be felt in the ether of the casino floor and would be an additional factor for the players. The congruous mirroring of gambling to real-life risk and reward cultivated numerology, astrology, and lucky charms to fit right in with the culture. Just as people sought divine guidance for prosperity, they found ways to accumulate wealth by using numerical vibrations to gain a statistical edge while gambling.

As these magickal methods became more customarily implemented into gambling strategies, uniformity of results emerged. The praxis of using occult magick in gambling was showing uncanny triumph. The success of people who followed the number combinations and energy affiliated with cards, suits, and colors as a baseline for tapping into a magickal combination for a winning gaming strategy through numerology became the subject of mass speculation, suspicion, and awe. In the design of many games, an advantage is usually given to the House or the odds against the player or players. These implications keep games from tying, establish betting orders, and inform players of the chance of winning vs losing. Manipulating the odds by understanding the numerical chances that exist as possible combinations was profound. From that starting point, people became devoted to finding ways to facilitate winning pots. They recognized that the vibrations of the numbers, combined with the elements in their environment, not only influenced their daily lives but had massive impacts on their gambling outcomes as well. When they realized they could influence their disposition, bodies, circumstances, and probabilities using natural elements in the physical realm, it wasn't difficult to transfer the same concepts to the spiritual realm. Therefore, every race, creed, religion, and nation has a colorful repertoire of winning gambling numbers, combos to avoid, numbers that bring negative energy, and different insights into gambling techniques. Re-stressing the individualistic nature of using magick in any gambling strategy.

As the gambling competitions evolved and became more sophisticated, so did the players, venues, and benefits of gambling. Gaming culture grew alongside, if not due to, the religious traditions, legal issues, and prosperity seekers of the decades. Entire empires materialized by utilizing gaming and gambling for civic involvement through collecting taxes and generating revenue with lottery incentives; common folk learned how to take advantage of their natural environment to wager their meager resources for the chance of gaining extraordinary wealth and philosophical and theological scholars used gaming for divination, fortune telling, math and science. The latter is the most impactful advancement for humanity. Gaming and gambling may have formed from sheer boredom, tinkering, tossing items, and asking questions of the Gods. History can't be sure, but what is certain is the mathematical and scientific developments the games and culture surrounding them encouraged. Numerology, astrology, and medicine weren't the only subjects enriched by the in-depth entanglement of people's gambling urges and civic development.

Numbers are the perfect tie to blend the mystic forces of nature with tangible developments that can be calculated and reproduced in the physical realm. Concepts such as probability, algebraic equations, mathematical laws, angles, time, physics, and geometry have ancient magickal origins that assemble our modern civilizations' literal foundation. People still benefit from the substantial habitat of buildings, roads, and other modern advancements they interact with daily, as well as the more abstract concepts they ponder internally to make sense of energy they feel but can't see. From asking the

Gods for divine guidance on acquiring wealth to creating tinctures with luck-attracting plants and elements, the benefits described in this guide for the contemporary gambler to explore and implement these numerical and sometimes scientific equations are verified by historical archives for all to see. Innumerable instances have arisen perpetually in human evolution where mathematical and theoretical advantages have influenced the circumstances. Stories abound of the indigent paupers of society ascending from rags to riches to prosperous, powerful kings taken to ruin by deceitful advisors to the growth of densely populated cities. A whisper of magickal or divine influence has been hidden underneath all of it. The most promising potential magickal strategy to guarantee consistent, dependable results will always be a combination that is spiritually and consciously aligned to the individual performing the task or expressing their intent.

# Superstition Vs Intent

The individual's results will be the most critical success metric for any gambling initiative. As discussed in the methods of magick, there are infinite combinations of winning magickal methods, numbers, and positive frequencies in the atmosphere to be utilized for prosperous gambling enterprises. On the contrary, much doubt and suspicion will be cast on the procedure if the results are less than satisfactory. In conclusion, repeating unrewarding outcomes perpetuates those vibrations, and success is never realized. Therefore, the question remains: how does one determine if the magickal technique they are implementing is thriving. For the answer to the question, let's go back to the definition of superstition. A superstition is defined as being a notion held despite evidence to the contrary or a false conception of causation. Magick, religion, mathematical concepts, and many scientific methods would fall under this broad definition of the word. In history, utilizing gambling magick would vary in acceptance through time as well. Before medicine, abstract mathematics, and navigation by the stars were adopted as standard practices by the citizens, they were regarded as superstition and unbelievable magick. These advanced concepts of traveling and mapping terrain, interacting with supernatural forces, and mixing cures from plants and elements did not transition well to individuals who did not subscribe to the discovery processes, usually those of limited education and mental capacity but also those hamstrung by a religious moral code. Factually, many magickal, mathematical, and scientific methods were being railed explicitly against in some religious organizations. As previously mentioned, moral code doctrines have been popping up since the beginning of gaming adaptation. The mixture of uninterested or directly opposed mindsets stymied a collective growth of positive connotations for evolving these magickal methods into commonplace in other areas of life, such as gambling. The consistent negative backlash for exploring psychic relationships in nature for gambling, gaming, and other prosperous gains pushed the study into the occult, despite even some religious organizations adopting their own acceptable extension of magickal dabbling.

Most of the magickal gambling advice will be found in the occult realm, which many people are still very wary of studying due to age-old stigmas. But some religious sects have holy saints, days, and other sacred numerical combinations in their texts that a sprinkling of devotees will utilize while gambling, too. Confirmed since the beginning of time, the separation of the people engaging in philosophical and analytical consideration of the world while trying to balance the desire to maintain a religious devotion to a deity created segregation in society's interpretation of psychic energy and other factors of the universe unseen by the naked eye. One side of the split adhered to the idea that divine intervention was the ultimate guiding force of nature; the opposition identified unique relationships and patterns in nature and explained the by-products of experimenting with them as extensions of the already existing power of nature. Still, not all so-called neutral parties were exempt from the actual practice of magick altogether. Sometimes, these individuals would be more persuaded by pragmatic folk magick traditions that were remarkably secular in nature or utterly void of obvious influential magick. It would seem it was just pure luck they had conjured a magickal gambling method, yet they would continue the act. Making that the actual definition of the word superstition, as opposed to the actual study of magickal gambling combinations. So, the confusion continues to mount as the debate continues. Neither side seems capable of producing enough palpable evidence to convince the other side of their progress. Consequently, this conundrum leads to much controversy in determining replicable results and their accuracy, especially when eminence depends heavily on a belief in the manner of execution.

Thus far, a hefty quantity of historical data is referenced in this manual concerning methods of magick, their origins, and notable practitioners, but the results are what this is really about. Therefore, another baseline establishment must be made. Aside from the religiously inclined spiritual or mystical forces, any manner of magick discussed in this aid for a winning gambling strategy can be backed by tangible methodology and the prosperity of thousands of people worldwide today. Or, in other words, physical cause and effect specific to an individual performing magick for intended results. Whether it be for the potential wealth gained by analyzing the next roll of the dice, betting against the Vegas odds, or hedging the stock market, a magickal pattern can emerge that shows a direct path to victory. Once an imprint of the solution becomes evident, an enlightened individual can repeat and reuse the tailored approach. To become cognizant of distinguishing patterns naturally reoccurring in the environment and to learn to profit from them, one should take prudent consideration of the world with an open mind, sharp senses, and education. Still, the simple task of accomplishing those goals is easier said than done. Internal and external factors can sincerely impact a magickal spell or ritual. When a procedure, ingredient, or phrase is repugnant to the caster, it will yield unsatisfactory results with less-than-acceptable lasting repercussions. Be mindful that the scientific laws of motion apply to all energy in the universe, including but not limited to magickal energy that may be implemented in conjuring gambling luck.

There are more ways for a magickal gamble to fall short than may be realized at first glance. Or, the letdown could possibly come from the fact that many do not accept the reality of the people's ability to influence their environment. There is really no way to be sure. Either way, the breakdowns of ineffective magick get the most attention when the matter is discussed. Triumphs can be easily waved off as coincidences, but failures are front and center of the argument against magickal intervention. There is always a skeptic in the crowd. Even worse, there are heretics who will shame and discourage any undertaking of magickal workings while, unbeknownst to them, they are participating in their own derivatives of magickal motions. Sadly, that happens frequently. People tend to excessively scrutinize methods and results intently when analyzing another individual's magickal connections, but not so much their own. It often leads to improper context and adjoining ideas that may have no connection at all. Another colossal misconception of causation to correlation to be contended with is the people who credit their magick to concocting an inherently coinciding natural event. People who refuse to acknowledge inevitable outcomes in their magick entirely do the most damage to the rationale. These doubts and misinformation could explain a lot of the defeat felt by people who have not been able to obtain the victory they seek attached to their magickal practices. The conclusions of those who do not know any better can be adversely manipulated by public opinion and create a negavitvity loop. Pessimistic feedback or disinformation can lead to a pattern of bad magickal combinations and will only have the chance to be prosperous if the cycle is corrected. Here is where a lot of souls will get trapped in the snare of gimmicks, tricksters, and charlatans. After multiple unfavorable outcomes, frustration and desperation can become a fever pitch, causing a line of disruption between desire, action, and results. Seeking an immediate turn of events, an individual is more open to adopting a method or course of action suggested by others who may have their own personal gain agendas in mind. A flimsy belief in cheaply obtained information, in addition to it perhaps being completely false, can also bring about an abundance of damaging outcomes. Not only for the person who uses the knowledge without understanding it thoroughly but also for the community of practitioners attempting to justify practical magickal effects.

As previously stated at the beginning of the chapter, and the reason for this guide being written, prosperity in magickal gambling must be a measurable metric to be justified. Otherwise, it would only be considered the mere observation of a superstition by textbook definition. Therefore, with all the overwhelming evidence routinely collected and aimed at the failures of magickal gambling, the chore of quantifying and substantiating the achievements of magickal gambling strategies can be a daunting principle to get behind. It's easier to write a book explaining what deity to perform a tribute to or how to cast a money spell to make a quick profit as an author, regardless of whether your reader reaps the benefits of their desires. Volumes on the topic are bountiful in the market and may have some truth in them but fail miserably to ultimately capture the foundation of why their particular approach is specifically favorable. Even fewer writers will express the importance of monitoring magickal progress in gambling meaningfully or how vibrationally connecting with the procedure can increase favorable outcomes. This is the driving factor that inspired the objective of this manual to be behind gathering and presenting the information in the tone it has set out. The aim is to accentuate unvarnished historical and empirical data while elaborating upon the impact of S.T.E.M advancements, religious contexts, and vibrational numerology theories. It must also express the effects of ignoring the existence of the physical restrictions of reality and how that will affect people's mental state. Magickal gambling success techniques are not trifling tasks that are done once in a lifetime and become the cure-all to every financial problem now or ever. That notion is unrealistic and ridiculous. Any personality or organization selling this thought process should be approached with a hefty grain of salt. Instead, the construction of magickal rites, talismans, or potions assumes thoughtful consideration of purpose, consequences, and results, including taking the time to learn about various aspects of life and mathematical logic that too many people neglect and take daily for granted. It also requires society and citizens to be aware of their energy and the vibrational power of the atmosphere, including the people within their vicinity. Magick entails the ability to read a room, feel empathy in particular situations, and connect with the potency of the elements of the ecosystem. Tuning a magickal knowledge to gain statistical advantages in monetary transactions of chance and probability will elevate a winning streak.

No matter the undertaking, whether it be mojo bags, spells, prayers, numerology, astrology, rites, rituals, blessed charms, or potions, there is always a paradigm to be uncovered and an amalgamation leading to luck to be constituted. As far as answering the question of verifying a successful magickal strategy, it depends solely on the purview and repercussions revealed in the life of the conjurer. The trajectory and by-products of the choices selected will be principal to the individual and, therefore, can only genuinely be analyzed for success by that individual, as each person will have their own outlook on each of the suggested processes of attracting luck for personal gain or wealth. Versatility is the most remarkable advantage of implementing magick in gambling. People were always mindful of this, as evidenced in their folk magick rituals and home remedies. Instinctually, society was drawn to what was available to them in their surroundings, and they used many varied assortments of those daily items to bring them luck. This infantile tinkering with materials eventually matured into an intellectual reflection that escalated introspections into realization. People became fascinated with understanding how they fit into the world, how their environment influences them, and if they were connected, whether they could change their own status in life. They employed the biological composition of the Earth to unlock fantastic material and extrasensory potential. Numerals and digits were fleshed out into formulas that translated abstract concepts and ideas into digestible patterns that could be identified by the common man. They used their knowledge to gamble in all areas of private or public life and in different occupational positions. Magickal gambling strategies were and continue to be applied to execute almost any desire as long as the fitting methodology can be deduced and impacts are consistently fruitful. Truth is, the technique has continued growing. In fact, people are still inventing new formulas of strategic magick for gambling every day.

Once psychology was established and used to express the advantages of the foresight of generating a magickal equation, the ability to gauge outwardly appearing randomized information and turn it into a calculated equation that could be solved with profitable results was quickly adapted. Outside of numerology, algebraic mathematics was an important tool that translated to magick as well as it did to mundane employment. An equation developed by Black-Scholes-Merton that rocked the foundation of the stock market in the 70's is a great example to highlight. Based on how the establishment of prices on the market was configured, an equation to hedge losses on buying and trading stocks that fluctuated in price was founded and implemented with never-before-seen gains over losses. Since the prices of stocks were constantly changing, the equation had to consider multiple factors to realize no loss, all profits more often than not. It operated so flawlessly the equation was an insider market enigma for years. Eventually, the magickal hot streak got loose, and the flaws in the original numerical sequences were polished and improved upon. Nowadays, every company has a unique footprint on how they hedge their losses on the market. Every investment has random potential to turn profits or send the stock into the red. The market's similarities to gaming propose an exciting opportunity to take these highly profitable equations and apply them to other gambling endeavors. The numbers of any game can be substituted into a similar style of mathematics that hedges bets to the favor of the better. The concept goes beyond simple card counting or betting within the odds ratio. This is literally identifying the winning combination and knowing when to take it. This magick formula doesn't have to remain shackled to the stock market either, as extensive applications have transpired throughout human existence; these techniques can be crossed over to suit almost any need.

Moreover, it is essential to realize the practice of magickal gambling isn't hampered by a meticulous rigmarole; instead, it gains boundless potential and increased opportunity through every venture. Since the modus operandi of execution varies so greatly from person to person, belief to belief, and really only the skeletal bones of the process are immutable, the soul's intentions become the only limitations. This means that individuals will use this knowledge to the extent their conscience allows, whether for perceived right or wrong. So, this is why the setup to this point was so extremely imperative to craft in the tone presented and also why scientific law is a more neutral perspective to discussing magickal outcomes and evidence of effect. This also keeps the language from discounting religious ceremonies and observances as they, too, can be substituted into the equation for success in magickal gambling. In conclusion, the efficacy of any attempts to interact with and manipulate the universe's energy or other astral forces will be dictated by the opinion of the individual or group performing the process.

# Ethical Dilemmas

Continuing with the idea that magickal intention is only prohibited by the person's desires, this brings us back to the point of ethical dilemmas. Most polite society presumes moral and immoral conduct and activities should be cut and dry. Nevertheless, when engaging in the occult exploration of psychic energy to attain an upper hand in gambling, virtue will be a contentious subject. For example, while constructing HooDoo, VooDoo, Witchcraft, or Folk magick mojo bags and lucky charms, each attribute to the amulet will be chosen with specific undertones implied. Herbs or natural earthen items such as pieces of precious stones, metal, and symbolic fabrics represent important significance and bear unique implications to every cultural custom and belief system on Earth. Commodities in gambling magick are chosen for their perceived ability to give rise to pulling energy from or attracting energy to the individual possessing the talisman. The person behind the strategy may believe that the items themselves are charged with the power to bring about the holder's intention, or they can believe that the items are taking the energy from the surrounding atmosphere. The difference matters.

A person who thinks the elements inherently hold power will probably have less ethical quandary over constructing and carrying a mojo bag or lucky charm, but someone who affirms the articles take energy from the environment may not find them very successful tools. Hence, how the same textiles can have differing effects per user. Invocations and incantations written by various religious groups and spell casters work in a very equivalent approach. Spells and rituals dictate, detail, and direct the intentions and outcomes of preternatural aspirations through vocal intent. Depending upon the language and foundation of the verbiage, ceremony and ritual have the potential to be the most offensive magickal technique to the practitioner's outcomes. Since oral commands only attract free-flowing energy or plead directly to a deity in some cases, it is much easier to have the potential for a conflict of interest when employing these strategies. Not all religious individuals will be open to appealing to the same entities, and some others will feel that taking energy that doesn't come to them naturally is immoral.

Potions can be another ethical crossroads. Elixirs, tinctures, and homebrews can command immediate changes in the atmosphere or the physical body through oral consumption, inhalation, or absorption through the skin. In this matter, the direct effects upon a person can be discriminated against as ethical or not. Some groups of people are nonchalant about the idea of experimenting with edible mixtures to induce various psychic effects, while others abhor the notion. Many attest that to remain effective in a gambling contest is to stay in control of oneself. Therefore, another use for such a potion could be realized if using the brew against an opponent was an option. That, of course, would depend on the individual and should highlight another often-discussed qualm. Should and can magickal workings interfere with others? Comprehending that all magickal exercises will reverberate natural effects through the ether will propel the concept of ethical morality through the equation. At some point, either a conflict with the individual's sincerely held religious beliefs, the origins of a magickal method, or the perceived interference with the natural balance will collide with that person's conscience and deter them from performing that particular task for luck or prosperity in gambling.

Numerology doesn't escape the ethical chopping block either, albeit for many of the same reasons discussed but also for unique explanations free-standing separately from the abovementioned consequences. Understanding the individual's conscience and how it feels about the mode and means of the magickal undertaking is the primary emphasis of ethical dilemmas. Comprehending the personal disposition of each ethical viewpoint of using magick for prosperity illuminates many ways manipulating betting can fumble the ball. Still, building this ability and wisdom also aids in assisting the conjurer in constructing a bond with their magickal ambitions. However, numerology does experience more open hostility than the rest of the other practices. Mainly because some strategies of using numerology in gambling are so successful that specific tactics have even been banned from casino floors. Card counting, slot machine watching, figuring out the probability of win percentages, hedging the losing odds vs the winning ones, and many more pattern-identifying behaviors can have a pit boss waiting to kick you from the establishment.

Many infamous individuals have actually been banned from major Vegas casino megaliths for life over these types of practices. The Nevada Black Book is exemplary evidence supporting this matter. Containing the names of well-known gangsters and mob bosses, the Nevada Black Book is one V.I.P.

list in Vegas no one wants to be on. The book was initially constructed in 1960, and it became the first inventory of individuals no longer welcome at gambling establishments due to discouraged behaviors or, as will be clarified, the assumption of cheating. It even contained the names of suspected illegal gamblers who were active prior to the conception of the collection of suspected cheaters. As the record grew from a small clutch of notorious mobsters, containing many names such as Sam Giancana, Michael Coppola, and Robert L. Garcia, to a whopping 35 names in 2018 when they added Las Vegas gambling addict Jeffery Martin, the register became more commonly known as the "List of Excluded Persons." Once penned in, dying is the only way to get off the list. Consider it one significant deterrence to cheating.

The names on the list of Nevada's Black Book have many charges against them; racketeering, slot rigging, book-keeping, and even using computer code to predict number combinations for winning bets. In the most notable cases, cheating is blatant and vulgar because mob tactics, by and large, are. However, other strategies unrelated to direct force or theft are still considered distasteful and can get you banned from a gaming establishment. This text encourages studying those frowned-upon gambling strategies and techniques through numerology that many casinos would consider unethical betting behaviors. In full disclosure, it is for this reason that ethical dilemmas have been included in the objectives of this book. Abnormal amounts of money were being won in those infamous cases, and it was happening very obviously one-sidedly, with a messy paper trail to boot. Nonetheless, the amount of money at stake isn't always what draws the immediate attention of the pit bosses and casino monitors; more often than not, it's the player's win percentage.

Winning at a higher percentage rate than expected is a huge red flag and will lead to extra eyes on the table to analyze the makings of the hot streak. The gambling games that are now today's most popular and well-played casino events have updated their outlined winning combinations and patterns based on detailed circumstances or randomized outcomes over the decades. Gambling complexity evolved alongside people's abilities to recognize simple patterns, so, over the eras, games revamped themselves into the luxurious and complex arenas now in existence. Game designers have adjusted rule sets, over/under percentages, payouts, and implemented many other tweaks to keep casino games as sporadic as possible and pattern seekers unable to use their abilities to win. Some notable updates include slot machines that use RNG, or random number generators, to produce random combinations; card games that have renewed rules for earning points from a 52-piece standard deck and that get changed out frequently during play; there is abundant book-keeping and betting for a variety of sporting events or animal races; there are new dice games, new wheel games, and don't forget the updated lottery, which implements air mix machines to shuffle plastic balls. Winning at a game of chance became as much a skill as it did a thrill. Thus, with the culture finding new, provocative ways to elevate gambling wagers, it was only natural that unscrupulous individuals and organizations would start exploiting those transactions.

As premised in the first chapter, the relationship between gambling and human nature, for better or worse, has pushed invention and ingenuity through the centuries. Unfortunately, on the opposite end of the spectrum, those with less-than-honorable intentions were also inspired by the potential profits of numerology in gambling. Reflecting back on the divergence of the social classes' gambling strategies, it is easy to see how the more mathematically inclined citizens were able to use their ability to analyze data to win more contests. They had a solid formula to show for it, while those using a more spiritual approach were flying under the radar of marketable success. Regardless, the win ratio percentage and reaction to the former are furthermore a testament to the power of numerology in particular. Cheating is technically breaking the rules by definition. Disputedly, precisely predicting the probability of the winning combinations and accurately betting when the odds are the best is, by right, the only way to win most games or bets. Casinos disagree, however, because if the approach is accomplished with any success, it can yield a high earning depending on the pot, consistency of use, and number of people employing the same techniques. In other words, the House can lose big.

In a struggle to combat the temptation of using enhanced playing methods, casino managers and other casual partakers claim that using logical prediction methods extracts the fun of the competitions, and the concept should just rely on the chance of the game. Herein lies more ethical conflict rooted in personal belief. Practitioners of numerology (who remain within the confines of the law) maintain that the main focus of entertainment for their competition is the mental challenge behind the superficial gimmick of amusement. The truth of the debate is in the eyes of the beholder, as mentioned in the previous chapter. If a magickal method does not infringe upon another, the perception of that method will be positive. Breaking the law is not a question of morality. Breaking the law in any fashion, for any reason, will lead to real legal consequences. Straightforwardly, fixing machines not to hit, skimming profits from the casino or bookie, adding extra cards to a deck mid-play, loading dice, stealing chips or money not within the gameplay, and threatening other players with violence, on the other hand, are very much considered out-and-out cheating. Not only are these activities guaranteed to get players 86'd from Vegas, but they're also illegal. Not many ethical dilemmas there.

Ethical dilemmas genuinely come under scrutiny when a person's conscience comes into play. Using numerology and magick in gambling is intoxicating and gives the individual an advantage that can influence the emotional vibrations in and around that person. How that person responds to the increased metaphysical vibrations will be judged for morality. As in the examples of the gamblers who found themselves on the blacklist, greed and the inability to control impulse behavior will be the downfall of any competition. Losing control is the equivalent of beating yourself. Those who fail to consider how others will receive their actions or, more importantly, those who cause direct harm to another person will be blindsided with natural repercussions. It must be accentuated that physical ramifications will still apply to a magickal maneuver if the desire is to manifest into reality. That's the point.

Other ethical factors such as sloth, envy, wrath, or greed also affect the aspects of magickal influence, and ramifications are not always contained to the person who cast the intention.

A sudden increase in class status due to a raise in salary, a flashy hot streak on the Roulette wheel, or catching every river card in a Poker game is going to raise some eyebrows and start a lot of conversations. Noticeable reverberations of winning streaks include crowds forming around tables in public venues, co-workers gossiping at work, and friends emerging more often with their hands out. Remembering the idea of balance in the universe, the fallout effect shows the theory's credibility that there is an equal but opposite reaction for every action. Even if a magickal strategy is wildly flourishing, public response to the streak can create jealousy and inspire covetousness, resulting in unhealthy interchanges with others. That is true at the moment of conception as well. Sometimes, regardless of whether or not a method of suspected cheating can be substantiated, anyone over-profiting from utilizing a magickal strategy will still be held responsible for their effects at the establishment's discretion. This can include being asked to leave a gambling platform. Being asked to leave is not the same as being put on "the list," but it can be embarrassing and ruin the vibe.

Any positive and negative vibrancy in the ether will affect the playing field. Not only will energy be generated through the excitement of players and the circumstances of the games, but it will also be attached to the existing environment, i.e., the physical building or betting application platform. This brings up another point to reference. Electronic items will emit more radio waves than a physical space, even if they are packed with other people, due to the metal components of technical devices and how they transmit data. It is essential to consider these radio waves and wifi signals as potential interference to directed magickal forces. Although wireless signals are technically ethically neutral, many people have found ways to affect the public's senses with noise frequencies, mood vibrations, and microwaves. Both governments and the general society have begun experimenting with these forces for profit, defense, and entertainment, not so privately in recent years. All of these facets have influenced the perception of ethically admissible conduct.

Psychic vibrations can be commanding extensions of human will, but as discussed, they also exist in nature and radiate from other people and animals on Earth. This illustrates precisely how dominating this energy can be and explains how vibrations affect moods unwittingly at times. When someone can assemble elemental forces and put them into motion, those supernatural intentions will do as they are directed. It can only behave literally as orchestrated by the construction. The after-effects of the enterprise will be the validation of how skillfully the strategy was planned. Ethical dilemmas arise when an actor does not consider all the outlying factors of magickal by-products. A lazy path of magick for prosperity or luck has the potential to create chaos on the astral plane of the source's immediate vicinity. The person may achieve the goal of their intention, but everything and everyone else around them appears to experience a drastic decline.

Last but not least, the most prevalent ethical argument against magickal gambling is the belief that exasperatedly exploiting positive energy vibrations creates a void in the surrounding environment. Due to the limited quantity of astral resources in the ethos, creating a vacuum of psychic power leads to many adverse reactions when crafting a strategy to draw luck. The moral principle for the individual is striving for balance with the environment. This mindset relies heavily on the idea that all the energy ebbing and flowing through people and the atmosphere is limited in this realm. Therefore, when an individual drains the power from the atmosphere at a rate it can not replenish, the natural result will be failure. Consequently, this is why many people who study magickal gambling strategies employ MoJo bags or charms to boost the luck in their vicinity. This circles back to the beginning; the ethical dilemmas in these instances will depend on the conjurer's will, their perception of religiosity, the physical consequences of immoral behavior, and the availability of vibrational energy in the ether.

# Grounding and Recycling Energy

Transitioning away from the ethics of magick, it is time to discuss specifically how magickal residue can operate and revert back to the cosmic pot after it is deployed in the mode expressed and formulated by the gambler. The universe surrounding us and everything contained in it is a gallimaufry of raw and cultivated elements. They are active magnetic components that prevail in everyday life. From start to finish, this publication has, and will continue to echo, the consistency of the population's consensus in favor of the existence of these supernatural facets of Earth. All previous chapters expound on the heterogeneous ideologies or religions that make up the consequential diversities edifying the actions of independent practitioners. This chapter will elaborate on the path of magickal intention or vibrational energy from source to purpose back to source. A widespread assumption is that irreconcilable dogmas can not coexist without disharmony, chaos, and unyielding power being wielded without control. Yet, by observing the world's habitually occurring designs, the opposite effect is often proven true. Natural laws do not tend to be irrational. The fact is that nature is logical to a fault and is held to strict rules governing reality. Behind the aura of the environment's randomness, a presence of either sentient design or rational outcome clearly exists as replicated motions have proportionate possible outcomes. Becoming familiar with various vibrations on the astral plane and having a basic idea of how they tend to act are skills that can be valuable to any gambler.

Regardless of the belief of where powerful celestial emanation initiates, the objective focus is that astral forces exist and, furthermore, can be controlled, influenced, and utilized. Mojo bags, lucky charms, potions, and numerology are examples of exerting and conducting the forces of nature deeply embedded in the universe. Each article put into a potion, charm, or Mojo bag has its own molecular composition based on the elemental makeup of the ingredient, and all of those items will have a unique vibe originating from them. When employed in magickal endeavors, numbers can express personalities, deities, emotions, or outcomes. Numbers can also be used to predict a winning day, time, or combination, creating positive energy, or they can send death warnings, omens, and losing streaks, detecting negative energy in the environment. Considering the ease of access to materials and the amount of knowledge being dispersed, there are limitless strategies to attempt, secrets to learn, and connections to the environment to be made. The chapters mentioned earlier narrate a linear connection between human evolution and magick, showing that the world continues to demonstrate recurring designs or vibes that become recognizable and capitalized on by the people. However, more work needs to be done that takes an expansive approach to the topic of magickal motion and grounding. This chapter will elaborate on how to raise that energy while crafting your amulets and rituals and then elucidate how to recycle it back into the ether. Many believe this practice is necessary to allow energy to remain active and influential.

The significance implied by hand gestures and body motions has been mentioned previously but has yet to be explained in detail. What makes physical motion a vital implication of magickal gambling? Well, motions impact the atmosphere because they resonate with vibrations. Material acts of collecting, constructing, or chanting require physical movement and motion in conjunction with mental contemplation regarding the materials. These movements create vibrations on the cosmic plane, intertwining with oscillations already in motion. Sometimes, energy can be met with interference or gain powerful surrounding forces mounting potency. Other times, it can be negated out. Vibrancy generated by magickal activity must still follow the scientific laws of motion. By implementing a logical extension, many concur when the energy produced is devised via positive intentions, the vibes are positive, and if not, vice versa. Hand signals, bowing, body movements, meticulous intoning, and asseverating words are potent magickal boosters when reining in astral forces. A multitude of gestures can re-enact an intention during spell work or direct the energy on how to move or where. Remember to keep in mind, however, that these actions can be quite evident if performed on the casino floor and can lead to illicit reactions from people in the vicinity, referring back to being banned based on perceived cheating. Active motions added to gambling strategies are physical means of raising energy and interacting with it on a level that can be experienced within the body. The intentions are then free to move about their directed path or attract and congregate with similar energy.

Some individuals do not have great poker faces. Gaining a magickal advantage or simply having a benefit above the rest can cause people to act out both publicly and inadvertently.

This creates an obviously high-energy situation and draws others in. Conversely, someone with a keen sensitivity to vibrational output can easily detect a losing table, anticipate a lousy hand, or the people in the facility could be exuding negativity effortlessly picked up on through their body language. This often leads to avoidance of an encounter or causes gamblers to move on from their current game. Human behavior is another aspect of life that can be misconstrued or misinterpreted based on the personal outlook of the individual making the observations and assumptions surrounding the intentions. Other times, people are utterly unaware of the vibrations they send into the atmosphere; this can cause confusion when another individual reacts to the person's energy instead of their physical interactions. A player's demeanor can arm an opponent with valuable information about the person they are analyzing. Body language can convey a message or vibrational energy without speaking; even eye contact can tell a silent tale. Some people are adept at reading rooms or profiling opponents based on the vibrations they send, and it can be quite an advantage. The exciting advantage of being surrounded by cosmic energy and astral vibrations in the ethos is the simultaneous engagement and equal availability gamblers can employ as magickal strategy boosters. Reading the room's vibrancy, learning to control the pulsations you emit, and recalling celestial power through magickal intentions are all formulas to move energy through the environment.

Using the scientific method as an outline, magickal formulas are easily understood. The route of astral vibrations moving from the originating source through the conjured elements used in a gambling strategy to realizing the desired outcome and, finally, how the energy inevitably returns to the source is cyclical. The process is familiar to people because our environment behaves in a mirror fashion. The seasons change in expected intervals, water cycles through the atmosphere in stages, and the sun rises and sets to rise again the next day. Natural operations bring repetitive outcomes that can be relied upon for consistency. Once a general cognition of how to commence from the premise of a scientific approach is confirmed, the process of designing a gambling strategy can begin. First, a hypothesis is constructed and designed with a specific purpose and desired outcome in mind. This will be regarded as a magickal intention. Remember to be exact with purposes and contemplate the unintended consequences should the desired result be achieved. Every action set in motion will continue on its course until it fulfills the purpose for which it was raised. This will indefinitely set off chain reactions along the way that should be accounted for, lest the results take an unexpected turn. This is also an essential step for recording progress. Having a good foundation and a strong follow-through will be imperative for success.

Next, a relation to the practice of magickal technique needs to be made. Based on the personal interactions with some of the previously mentioned forms of constructing lucky magickal amulets, spells, and winning numerical sequences, the magickal gambler should establish a routine they are comfortable experimenting with and have a basis of belief in. Establishing a bond between the ingredients implemented in lucky charms, having faith in the mode of execution, and the state of mind of the individual tapping into them for their advantage will decide whether the endeavor will succeed. If the person crafting the magickal strategy does not believe in the power behind the methodology, then the technique will go awry. The ingredients will behave as their metaphysical composition dictates, regardless of the individual's beliefs, and this can work favorably if executed well or poorly if not even considered as a possibility. The general recommendation of this book is to explore the various cultural, religious, or folk magick approaches to gambling strategies instead of following a trendy gimmick. The ultimate goal when using magick in gambling is to construct a winning streak with replicable results. The best way to achieve that goal is to be completely comfortable and educated about what is happening on the astral plane and how that affects the physical realm.

Finally, the most often disregarded step in crafting a magickal gambling technique is intentionally grounding or gradually decelerating left-over energy after it has satisfied its purpose. This idea may sound counterproductive, as most astral movement is explained mainly as being projected outwardly through the individual's directed will. However, keeping in mind that the psychic pipeline both receives and sends these frequencies, the fact is that an echo of reverberation will return to the sender and needs to escape back to its natural source. In other words, an action or intent sent in motion will achieve a result that will elicit a return reaction to complete the cycle. The job isn't complete until the entire revolution of effort, from the preparation to climax to rest, has been concluded. The whole trajectory of the energy will determine if it will benefit the gambler or receive interference and possibly return reversely. Plenty of gamblers also operate under the impression that ensuring the positive energy collected and received goes back to the source means that the same energy has the potential to be re-tapped for later retrieval. Which is a common thought when storing magickal talismans and mojos. Many owners of these lucky charms store them in ceremonial bags, on altar tops, or wrapped in a protective cloth until they are actively used in an effort to keep the magick from draining too quickly. The idea of keeping this energy in circulation is the conclusive motion of magick.

Deceleration and grounding are two popular methods of returning energy from where it came, but they are not the only methods available, and they operate differently. Deceleration is defined as the reduction of the speed at which something is moving. In this case, we are talking about reducing the amount of time it takes for collected energy to naturally leech back into the environment. Deceleration operates differently from grounding because, as continuously discussed, it is a built-in behavior of energy to remain in motion and return to its source. Grounding is the spiritual intention of the practitioner to return residual energy to its source. A person who raises and communes with the vibrational astral power on a physical level, using their bodies more so as their conductors, will need to shed that magickal high back into the ether. Not only does the energy tend to drain from the body just as it does from an object, but the individual experiencing the rush is literally influenced by the forces they summoned. The dynamic of control can change rapidly when conjuring lucky energy. Therefore, the key is to take advantage of having the authority over the elements while that tactic is available and create scenarios that encourage the same resource to be prepared to be used again. If the method is carried out advantageously, it is appropriate to record the results, enabling the fruitful endeavors to be examined for future analysis. By implementing this scientific approach to magick, gamblers will have a more victorious winning streak that they can employ under any circumstance. The more often they complete their magickal cycles, the more they replenish their own pot of wealth.

The entire premise of using magick in gambling is to gain better control of the game's outcomes and encourage a winning streak, but care must be taken to achieve that goal without triggering an adverse reaction. Studying the Earth's natural processes to construct a magickal cycle for energy to gain potential for prosperity and retrieve it for the conjuror is equivalent to adding a turbo booster to a car. Now, before people start heading to Amazon and hitting the "Buy it Now" button on any old turbo booster, they check to see if it fits the vehicle. Once an applicable selection is made, it must be prepared, installed, and maintained. The turbo should not run while the auto's engine is off and should not be run excessively, or it will burn out and damage the machine. Magickal gambling strategy is no different. Some approaches will not fit the model and should be swapped for better performance; other methods will work so well that they will have more potential to be abused, thus potentially damaging the individual or their realities in the process. The keys really rest in the hands of the individual who drives the vehicle in both scenarios.

Grounding and decelerating power is also the same as shutting off and idling a vehicle's engine. It is done to save gas and preserve the machine's and parts' functionality. Everybody knows that cars can't drive forever, and they need regular maintenance to operate efficiently. Not every vehicle operates the same way, so manufacturers found constructing an owner's manual worthwhile. People could consult it from time to time to ensure proper maintenance is completed, and from there, a log of scheduled upkeep is kept to record the progress. Moving energy through objects, motions, or thoughts is much like the gas moving through the automobile engine. If the tank is full of quality gasoline and the engine's pistons are lubricated, the machine will run well; if these ingredients are subpar or the machine is not in good condition, it will not run. Considering the rise of today's gas prices, this metaphor will stress the importance of reserving that tank by any means necessary. Thinking of magickal energy in this way will encourage all to deploy more responsible uses and applications of the practice during a betting wager and give them access to more resource material than ever thought relevant to the task through introducing the long-standing cultural chronology of the craft.

Essentially, the bottom line to delivering a successful magickal gambling strategy is knowledge, discipline, and intent. Having the proper formula, however, doesn't guarantee success. Every magickal project must be realized entirely and be permitted to run a complete cycle. This requires individuals to control themselves and have an insightful perspective on what could result from their actions. A good magickal strategy can go A.W.O.L. if the person playing the game becomes emotionally overwhelmed. Doubt, fear, anger, and distrust are obviously negatively impactful and will not help win gambling endeavors, but riding a conjured hot streak that has run out of gas can be equally inadequate. As stated in the previous chapters, magickal gambling can benefit gamers, giving them insights and luck for their winning strategies. Still, starting out by winning big and then losing suddenly can leave an intoxicating high and cloud one's better judgment, making it even more essential to know how to read the environment's energy, stay in control, and know when to walk away or seek help.

# Acknowledging Problems

As much as everyone likes to win, and despite the fact that they will always try to find different ways to engage lucky charms and attract wealth to themselves, the topic of losing must be addressed. Persisting to the heart of the matter, it is imperative to understand that it is impossible to win without ever losing, and the energy surrounding a loss can be reverberative. People's reactions to unsuccessful wagers are as critical to outcomes as researching and constructing a preternatural gambling approach that resonates with the individual. The psychic energy the player brings to the gambling plan through their magickal strategy or by implementing other psychic forces already existing in the ethos doesn't randomly assemble by chance. They are drawn there purposely and with intention. All cosmic radiation has a source, whether the supernatural foci originate from previously collected energy in a lucky charm, spell, or potion or if they derive from an aggregation of energy from other gamblers. An incalculable number of consistently fluctuating vibrations are always at play when dealing with humanity, as individual desires vary from person to person. These emotions can cause a disturbance in the field of energy flow. Addiction, greed, jealousy, anger, and fraudulence are just a few of the opposite intensities of positivity that counteract the type of energy sought for productive gambling methods originating from human emotions.

Powerful emotions hugely impact gambling wagers when they become visibly hostile physical animations or invisible pessimistic personality barometers. Every individual creates vibrational energy in their space through their actions and demeanor, and the intense feelings of a person can disseminate, affecting others. This type of energetic interference with the aura of the betting atmosphere is exclusive to human intervention and results from their interactions with life situations. Sentient beings reacting to environmental changes in or around them is a different pulse than the exuberance experienced from a source of nature. Human energy is experienced on the psychic veil differently than the type infused in elemental composition. It is usually easily recognizable because it is primarily responsible for causing deviations from otherwise predictable outcomes. Sometimes, disruptions occur because subconscious intuition is ignored for the worse. Straightforwardly, instincts are at the root of human emotions, help establish social constructs, and provoke reactions from man's ecosystem. They are integral to survival and handy for enacting a healthy approach to magickal gambling, enabling man to identify beneficial situations or avoid costly ones. Humans have a penchant for manipulating their environment to cater to their feelings. Based on the facts of any given exchange, people are customarily conditioned to respond in a predetermined manner, and mortal behavior has exhibited predictable habits since the dawn of time. Therefore, instead of arguing for or against a divine explanation or defecting to a godly discretion for these interactions, where many may lose or find their own revelations, people must first confront the undeniable reality of the power that can be gained through mastery of human restraint and familiarity with psychological balance.

Human behavior is an inevitable obstacle that will be encountered while attempting to engage in wagers and magick advantageously. It is the least predictable variable for magickal gambling and must be internalized as much as externalized. Sizing up the competition is step one when walking into a match-up, but the player has the potential to be their own worst enemy as much as their worthy opponent. It should be standard practice for everyone to be aware of their personal vulnerabilities in order to set realistic expectations and monetary boundaries to which they hold themselves accountable. This may include plans to walk away after a certain win-loss ratio, a particular numerical dollar amount, or type of experience with other players. Honing the art of scrutinizing and controlling personal behavior can be used to take advantage of all situations on the casino floor. Personal demeanor is built on a two-sided coin in and of itself. One side is self-experience, which denotes all one can see, touch, taste, and sense. Self-awareness and interpretation of the world are the ego factors in this dynamic—in other words, the confessed provocation behind the enactment of events or desired outcomes. This is humanity consciously acting in the moment with purpose. The other side of the coin is what an individual reciprocates to their atmosphere, otherwise considered the Id or sub-conscience. People may be less aware of this portrayal of themselves to the public, but their motions are subject to analysis or retort from their peers, nonetheless. All actions, even subtle eye movements or covert agendas, have tangible repercussions on the physical realm and continue a cycle of reaction from the environment, including responses from other people in the area. This anecdotal concept of the perpetual circular motion of events demonstrates that even human conduct can be construed to follow basic scientific principles, such as every action has an equal but opposite reaction.

Expanding on this crude scientific logic, everyone has been told that positive emotions tend to spread and attract optimistic personalities, and it is assumed that negative feelings and actions are inclined to attract pessimistic personalities. However, this idea is not confined to kindergarten classrooms; it also extends to magick and vibrations. Part of creating a prosperous gambling strategy is creating a winning atmosphere. Gamblers who surround themselves with objects, situations, or people antithetical to their moral or esteemed principles will not reap equally prosperous benefits by engaging in the similar behaviors of their peers, no matter the number of victories they observe people to have with the same materials or methods. For example, red isn't everyone's lucky color, and only some gamblers consider the number thirteen a jinx. The productivity of the gaming method depends heavily on the disposition of the gamer and how they handle a loss. The appearance of an individual's failure with a popular method of luck contrary to that which others have implemented with favorable results can turn into a series of disappointments that build upon themselves. In these cases, it has nothing to do with the magickal method and everything to do with the individual. This is why it is a requirement to remain in total control of a gambling endeavor. There are many dubious traps and charlatan tricks to encourage a weak-willed player to extend themselves beyond their means or make them fall prey to deceptive scams.

Bad juju (hexes, curses, or ill-will afoot), cheaters, and con artists can be challenging obstacles for the gambler to contest with, and at times, it will feel like every lucky ritual gets negated. Roguish individuals or wildcards can create uncertain tangents in the logical path of events that interrupt otherwise smooth-flowing energy. Unprincipled practitioners can cross the line from legal to illegal activity without thinking twice if the money is right, and people who feel they have nothing left to lose can act out and proceed with untenable conduct that hurts them more than it helps. Peer pressure, mounting monetary debt, or family issues can cloud a person's judgment or create grey area scenarios for some individuals that cause them to act in ways that are contradictory to their prosperity. Inherently, the initial reaction while experiencing these tragedies if engaging in magickal gambling is to blame the magick and gambling strategy. Generally, the consensus would agree that this is the appropriate place to start, but if the continuous failure persists even after adjusting a magickal gambling strategy, it is time to self-examine behavior.

Personal feelings often lead to people creating repetitively negative scenarios for themselves. It is frequently referred to as being stuck in a rut or being on the downslide. The perception of owning no luck or retaining lousy luck is usually the motivation for a person to attempt to use magick to gain an edge in gambling in the first place. This inspiration is misplaced from conception and bears the brunt of the blame for poor execution. Thinking that an easy route to financial freedom exists via one simple spell is a fool's folly. Anybody who looks at magick as a quick fix for a severe problem will be disappointed with their results and spread shoddy information about their endeavor. The worst part is that they will remain in their unfortunate situation and generate negativity surrounding the craft of magickal gambling. A thoughtful gambler comprehends magick is a strategy booster, not a golden ticket. Sadly, it shows people are more willing to try to influence everything they can in their environment to gain luck except their behavior. Most of the time, that is their real issue and the only way for them to improve from their current position. Ultimately, the biggest win is when the gambler realizes the significance of learning that humanity is restricted to what it can perceive and how people react to those perceptions.

All volitions set into motion must come full circle, and people influence all atmospheric vibrations through their actions. Behaviors can increase or kill the length of a hot streak. Actions speak much louder than words and give off noticeable vibes others can pick up on. This makes it easy for a seasoned gambler to avoid situations that may not be profitable to them or for a hustler to find a target. Harboring or displaying pessimistic behaviors will drive away positive individuals and habits, making it hard to relate with them and the energy they bring with their personalities or luck charms. Subconsciously, gamblers in this situation limit themselves and don't even realize it. Any positive energy they could swing into their vicinity may be compelled to avoid them at all costs, or a more assertive player may choose to capitalize on them in a vulnerable situation. Either way, the gambler can only control their response to the situation they find themselves in. The power move is knowing the correct answer: walk away now. The warning signs are being aware that all the lucky preparations made before the game no longer bring prosperity to the gambler. The best bet in this case is to live to fight another day.

It isn't always obvious when to walk away from the table for individuals on a brutal losing streak. There are many people who exhibit addictive personalities that overstay their fortunes welcome in the casino playroom. The House will never decline a paying customer, and they openly market practices to entice players to stick around. For instance, there are flashy game names and bright blinking lights, free libations, and captivating people. Mobile devices even boast the convenience of gambling at any time, in any place. Numerous detrimental factors can corrupt gamblers' intentions and clear thinking in the gaming sphere, making it challenging to end the game. Alcohol, sex, availability, and self-popularity, just to name a few. People can be as addicted to the atmosphere of a casino as they are to the game for profit. The difficulty of identifying the root of a gambling issue is increased when these existential indicators are considered on top of the potential for monetary gain. Temptations can even be scapegoated as grounds for individuals to be addicted to gambling. For whatever reason, there are times when the conduct becomes detrimental to the person and their environment. Therefore, alongside a magickal plan, create a network of friends and family who will speak up if they see signs of addiction and take the time to learn how to be that one to speak up to a peer if necessary.

It may be the most formidable discussion that anyone will have concerning a subject that is supposed to be amusing and profitable, but when a gambler can not walk away from the table, they may need intervention. Addiction isn't a straightforward issue to deal with, and there are no whimsical magickal cures that exist to deter it from devastating lives. This is why it is fundamental to begin every gambling enterprise with a healthy mindset, remain comfortable with any magickal method chosen to operate with, and impose limitations before entering any betting wager. Still, the best-intentioned gamblers can get swept away by human emotion and fall victim to substance dependence, obsessive behavior, or tremendous loss of physical property, such as their house or their vehicle. The potential for an individual practicing a magickal strategy for gambling to be more vulnerable to these pitfalls may even be higher than the average player. A medically reviewed article from 2017 in HealthLine cited the National Council on Problem Gambling's percentage of Americans with a known gambling issue at two percent of the population, but those individuals are not categorized by gambling method.

Obviously, there isn't a published allocation of the magickal community's specific demographic ratio of problem gamblers, making it impossible to recognize gamblers addicted to magick, per se. However, the intoxication of experiencing a sense of presentiments that grants advantages over others is a determined psychological disorder in some narcissists. Still, this isn't the only acknowledged classification of mental impairments that would be more inclined to develop addictive behaviors related to combining gambling and magick. There is an epidemic of people who grapple daily with merely controlling their weak impulses. People who can not control themselves will not have the efficacy to achieve prosperous results in gambling with magick or otherwise because this methodology requires strict discipline and education. Dual co-factors such as high-risk personality types co-opting with high-risk entertainment should be a red flag that prompts the gambler to take extra precautions while betting. Magick is experienced as having the power to influence the environmental elements or vibrational energy in the world and being the one employing them for beneficial means. This can be overwhelming to a delicate disposition. When individuals who are predisposed to psychological personality disorders practice magickal gambling, it may exacerbate an underlying illness.

Once an issue is pinpointed, the subsequent task is finding suitable resources to acquire assistance to rectify the problem. Remember, this can be a depressing and isolating experience, even if a support system is in place. Addicts may have anguish over admitting there is a problem, and many try to conceal the seriousness of their dire strains. Inevitably, gambling addicts also habitually endanger their family's well-being with their actions as well. The effects of an addiction can be far-reaching and withstanding, which makes the matter that much more complicated to sort out. An addiction that has become life-altering for an individual signifies that seeking external aid is appropriate because the situation has become out of control. Fortunately, no one has to endure this painful, emotional ordeal alone, even if that person fails to assemble a preemptive safety net of an extended support system. Vast networks of professionals are available to listen, evaluate, and advise anyone seeking assistance in breaking a gambling addiction. Similar to the pursuit of magickal knowledge, there are tips and tricks that experts in the field of behavior and personality analysis can give to the person who seeks insight. They will work confidentially provided the situation does not pose an immediate threat of harm to the patient or others, and they are typically experienced in handling any complex addiction problem. If anyone is experiencing issues with addiction, please call Gamblers Anonymous International Service Office, 1306 Monte Vista Avenue, Suite 5, Upland, CA 91786.

Phone (909) 931-9056.

# Mr. Big's Charms

A charm is an object that brings luck; it's also a quality of being attractive and pleasing. There are several types of charms, but they mainly relate to attraction and good luck. A lucky coin is a charm.

Christian Charms Holy Objects

Saint *Medals;* My recommendations: Saint Cajetan Saint Of Gambling is also used to help overcome Gambling addiction; if you think you need help, please connect GAMBLERS            ANONYMOUS            Toll-Free            at 1-800-GAMBLER

Saint Jude is a Saint for impossible causes, like playing Poker with others better than you are, and you know it. Mary herself gave us the Miraculous Medal in the 1830s. It is not a good luck charm, per se, but worn around the neck, it may guide you if you remain open to that guidance. I have all three around my neck, and I never remove them.

The Bible

One of the most influential books for aid or protection is The Bible. There are many ways to use this book for protection, even if you are starting your day.

I find that starting out saying Psalms 91 keeps me in a good space vs. allowing my anxiety to take over. Trust me, much time playing in a Casino, being controlled by your anxiety will be a bad thing, from making the wrong decision at the Blackjack table to thinking about chasing your losses a lousy choice.

Psalms 34:4: "I sought the Lord, and he answered me; he delivered me from all my fears." No, He will not tell you the winning lotto numbers. Having this verse on my person again helps me keep my mind clear, which is vital when you're in risky events.

Before going out to gamble, read Psalms 34.8 as you drink a glass of water.

For Slots, recite Job 20:18

phylactery (charms). Durga Charm protects you from the evil loss of money. Put in your Mojo Bag. Mercury Dime has silver content if you can get one minted in the year of your birth. It's hard to do since I quit minting them in 1945. Note that the ones minted in 1916 are said to be very lucky. Put in your Mojo Bag. A horseshoe charm is helpful if you are doing sports betting. In or attached to your Mojo Bag. Three acorns are essential for your Mojo bag; you can find them in most parks/woods. Look for Oak Trees

# Mr. Big's MOJO

You can buy them online if you follow the directions they should come with. (Note that it is terrible luck to have a member of the opposite sex handle even look upon your Mojo Bag.) My kin made our own. Others around the area where my great-aunt lived would have my aunt make one for them, most of them for gambling. A few law enforcement officers would have her make one to use for protection. The type of mojo I will discuss here is used for gambling. Most supplies can be found in Jo-Anne Fabrics stores, Hispanic neighborhood grocery stores, or online. The cost to make one other than the Florida Water Hoyt's cologne should be less than $20. The time needed depends on your sewing skills. It would be best to make this talisman during the waxing moon (the moon going from New To Full). The best day of the week for this task is Friday. Using green cotton cloth about 7" on a side, make a pouch ( a drawstring closer is nice, but you can also tie a firm knot to close it when the time comes. In the bag or the center of the cloth, before you close it up, place A two dollar bill on the face side of the bill and put a bit of Hoyt's cologne or Florida Water. A mercury dime. A bingo card or lottery ticket, three acorns, a lodestone, or a pinch of magnetic sand. As you do, recite Psalm 90: 17. After completion, this step is done; as you close the bag, exhale three times, "giving the bag life." Put a bit of Hoyt's cologne on the bag itself. Place the bag in a location where others can not see or handle it; otherwise, you will lose the bag's power. Should a woman hold the bag, you will come under her control.

My Kin's Mojo Story

During the 1950s, around Rock Springs, WI, there was a Ku Klux Klan group that would gather around and cause trouble before I was born or my Dad/Mom was married. My maternal side, being black from the Appalachians, knew the trouble the Klan would be, and let's say law enforcement was not up to the task: my Grandfather and his brother (my great-uncle). The story goes that my great-aunt made them Mojo bags of protection. After conducting a Moon protection ritual, the brothers walked into the next meeting with tire irons and a sawed-off shotgun to wish the thugs farewell. The Klan never came back to Rock Springs. During my childhood, everybody told this story once Jack came out. It is just a story. There is proof the Klan did come to Rock Springs, and one day, they vanished. There are worse things to use dark magic on than protecting your Kin. Perhaps my Uncle paid the price with his mind.

# Mr. Big's Numerology & Magick Squares

The policy is another word for the numbers racket, where a player would pick a set of numbers, pay a fee, perhaps as small as a dime, and win if that number was correct for that day. A dine would win possibly$100. A good payoff when, in the 1920s, a dollar a day was good pay. When the Great Depression hit, a dollar a day was excellent pay, very much so in the poor areas of Cities. Friendly for the mob was policy was easy to set up and run, customers would come to you, plus at the bar every candy story you ran your game from, you could also offer other services from Hookers to a juice loan. You can't beat a business where many of your customers come to you. An enterprising number runner ( a guy picking up the bets, giving out the winners) could easily make $100 a week, making him a well-off man of means in an area where many may not have steady work, a man who wants to feed his family, running numbers was an excellent way to do so. There was little fear of getting caught if you were a small fine or had a night or two in jail. Sometimes, a runner was also beaten and robbed, compared to, say, Rum Running, which was very low risk until the mob wanted in. When the mob, either the Jewish gangs in New York or the Outfit in Chicago, saw the amount of wealth the numbers were making, first, they would try to buy out the black Policy banks. If that did not work (Chicago being the prime example), it would rub them out so the mob could talk them over. The last significant Black Kingpin to be gunned down, Tony Roe, was killed in

Chicago in 1952. The other major Black number kingpins fled to Mexico. From the late 1800s to about the 1930s, a line of books was written on how dreams can be used to pick your numbers. Advertised in Black-owned newspapers, they were rather good sellers. However, the decline of neighborhood papers also meant this type of guidebook dropped. I have not seen one, even in a library, in decades.

Lucky Numbers

Most have, luckily, numbers we first used growing up, such as 7, just because we liked it. In my case, 3 gets attention because I have three sisters, all three years apart. Numbers I do well to avoid in life are 2 and 11. You have to track the numbers in your life that have meaning. In the West, numbers like thirteen are considered "unlucky." Numbers like 13 have to do with Christian thought, 11 for the loss that is incurred playing Craps. When that number comes up, roll the dice. In Asia, numbers with repeating digits, such as 777, are lucky; each culture worldwide has unique number guidelines. Is any number truly unlucky? Most likely not, but if you think a number is for you, then you should use it. If it feels unlucky, you can stay away. A Bible Verse to recite to perhaps dream of lucky numbers for the lottery.

Psalms 89: 19-21: Use your name vs David. It's best to keep a pen and paper to record messages you receive.

Magic Squares have a history long before Christ's birth in China and England. Speaking of England, Magic Squires would hold quite the place in Alchemy. It is said that Sir Isaac Newton studied the creation of the squires to help him invent calculus and his experiments in Alchemy.

The best use of Numerology is in Magic Squares, where numbers in a grid add up to the same number, be it access or diagonally.

The best one to carry as I do pinned to the inside of my jacket

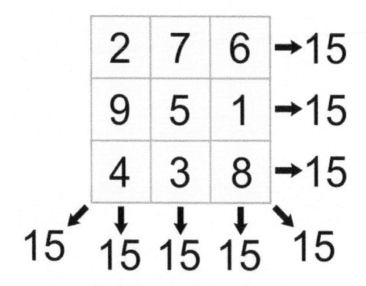

Another is if you play Mahjong

| 9  | 2  | 25 | 18 | 11 |
|----|----|----|----|----|
| 3  | 21 | 19 | 12 | 10 |
| 22 | 20 | 13 | 6  | 4  |
| 16 | 14 | 7  | 5  | 23 |
| 15 | 8  | 1  | 24 | 17 |

Order=5x5

Sum=65

Numbers have great power, as anyone who has had to do a tax return can tell you.

# Mr. Big's Tips and Tricks

Keep a piece of bay leaf in your left shoe.

Keep a nutmeg in your left pocket when playing dice.

If you are going to play cards, use Hoyt's Cologne. Failing that, substitute Florida water before sitting down to play.

When buying lottery tickets, keep moss with you. Place the moss ON TOP of the ticket (until drawn or you wish to scratch them off)

Are you playing the slots? Recite Job 20:18 before playing. After playing for over a few hours at a Casino or any time spent in Vegas, please do a raw egg bath.

A) Take a raw egg

B) Pass the egg around your body, starting at the feet on one side and ending at your feet on the other side.

C) As you do so, imagine negative energy going from you into the egg.

D ) Dispose of the egg in the trash and wrap it in newspaper.

DO NOT BREAK THE EGG !! Tossing the egg in running water like a river is the best way to do this. If the egg wash is not for you, a warm bath in which you add kosher salt will also do the trick.

# Conclusion

You put all the money down on this wager; it's the last gamble of the night. The call rings out over the crowd, 'Hold on all the bets!' You just made it. The dealer grabs the chunky red dice and, *THWAP*, throws them. The dice fly swiftly hit the table and go to each end, tipping and tumbling across the flats. The assemblage roars in excitement. The energy in the room is palpable. The cubes smack off the bank of bright green felt, changing direction and motion. Abruptly, a flat side of each jumping square clings to the board, and they slide to rest with a final numerical digit represented on their dotted faces. What number did they read for you? If you implemented a unique magickal strategy inspired by Mr. Big's Magickal Guide to Gambling, the probability is highly likely that your winning number hit precisely as you planned. You may even have some recycled energy stored and waiting to ensure you never leave the casino broke again. We hope you're not only repetitively successful with some luck left over but also convey the wealth of knowledge you've gained with all your friends. Don't be rich and lonely; there's plenty of prosperity to share.

Now that you can articulate why people are less likely to use magick in gambling, you can feel the vibrations in the atmosphere around you, and you have a great idea of where to find ingredients for your next mojo bag, you're ready to take this show on the road and ante up with the big dogs. You know that gambling and human nature go hand in hand, and no one will intimidate you with a big bluff. You'll be reading the energy of the table and recognizing numerical patterns in the games like a pro, so taking home a winning pot will be second nature to you. Everyone will notice your confidence when you invite them to the next poker game, and they'll be trying to figure out your technique all night long. You won't feel ashamed telling them you read Mr. Big's Magickal Guide to Gambling and found your personal hot streak generator. Then, after the game, let them know where they can get a copy of their own. Anyone can make a magickal gambling strategy they feel confident using in any wager.

# Bibliography

Adminwhi. "The History of Lottery Games." *Whitefeatherdiaries.Org* -, 19 Nov. 2022, whitefeatherdiaries.org/the-history-of-lottery-games/.

Association of Independent Readers and Rootworkers. "Category:Mojo Bags." *Category:Mojo Bags - Association of Independent Readers and Rootworkers*, 2024, readersandrootworkers.org/wiki/Category:Mojo_Bags.

Astrocult. "A History of Numerology: From Roots to Modern Times." *AstrOccult.Net - Your Best Vedic Astrology Guide*, 2024, astroccult.net/history-of-numerology.html#google_vignette.

August 15, 2023 | Emma Cieslik | Comments. "Appalachian Folk Magic: Generations of 'Granny Witchcraft' and Spiritual Work." *Smithsonian Center for Folklife and Cultural Heritage*, 2024, folklife.si.edu/magazine/appalachian-folk-magic.

Bajaj, Sheelaa. "History of Most Famous Numerologist - Sheelaa m Bajaj Celebrity Numerologist." *Dr. Sheelaa M Bajaj Celebrity Numerologist & Tarot Card Reader*, 27 Mar. 2023, sheelaa.com/most-famous-numerologist-in-history/.

Barras, Colin. "Is This the Original Board Game of Death?" *Is This the Original Board Game of Death? Ancient Egyptian Senet Board May Signal Shift from Mere Pastime to a More Serious Game*, 6 Feb. 2020, www.science.org/content/article/original-board-game-death?rss=1.

Brilliant, .org. "Black-Scholes-Merton." *Brilliant Math & Science Wiki*, 1 Jan. 2024, brilliant.org/wiki/black-scholes-merton/.

Britannica, The Editors of Encyclopaedia, "game." "History of Gambling." *Encyclopædia Britannica*, Encyclopædia Britannica, inc., 23 Jan. 2024, www.britannica.com/topic/gambling/History.

Cassar, Claudine. "How Mafia Organizations Use Rituals as a Weapon." *Anthropology Review*, 2 Mar. 2023, anthropologyreview.org/anthropology-explainers/how-mafia-organizations-use-rituals-as-a-weapon/#google_vignette.

Chaldean Numerology, ondCode.fr [online website]. "Chaldean Numerology Calculator - Online Name Number." *Calculator - Online Name Number*, 2024, www.dcode.fr/chaldean-numerology.

"Cheiro." Edited by Project Gutenberg, Internet Archive, Internet Speculative Fiction Database, Library of Congress, with 44 library catalog records, *Wikipedia*, Wikimedia Foundation, 19 Feb. 2024, en.m.wikipedia.org/wiki/Cheiro.

Commonwealth of Massachusetts. "Massachusetts Gambling Impact Cohort Study (Magic)." *Massachusetts Gambling Impact Cohort Study (MAGIC) | UMass Amherst*, 2024, www.umass.edu/macohort/.

Cooper, Ben. "Game Theory in Christian Perspective-Cooper." *The Association of Christian Economists*, 13 June 2016, christianeconomists.org/2015/06/01/game-theory-in-christian-perspective-cooper/.

Doughty, Susan. "Classics & Ancient History Warwick Classics Network." *Just a Game? An Ancient Dice Tower and Roman Society*, Paul Grigsby, 30 Aug. 2022, warwick.ac.uk/

fac/arts/classics/warwickclassicsnetwork/publicengagement/studentengagement/storiesofobjects/blog/vernon/.

The Editors of Encyclopaedia, The Editors of Encyclopaedia. "Numerology." *Encyclopædia Britannica*, Encyclopædia Britannica, inc., 15 Jan. 2024, www.britannica.com/topic/numerology.

Efforts of Magick. "An Easy Folk Magick Money Ritual." *Efforts of Magick*, 6 June 2021, effortsofmagick.xyz/wealth/89-an-easy-money-ritual/.

Encyclopædia, Britannica. "Prelude to the Han." *Encyclopædia Britannica*, Encyclopædia Britannica, inc., 2024, www.britannica.com/place/China/Prelude-to-the-Han.

Esparza-Reig, Javier, et al. *Health-Related, Social and Cognitive Factors Explaining Gambling Addiction*, 30 Sep. 2023, www.ncbi.nlm.nih.gov/pmc/articles/PMC10572556/.

Gamblers, Anonymous. "About Us." About Us | Gamblers Anonymous, 2024, www.gamblersanonymous.org/ga/content/about-us.

Gambling.net. "The History of Gambling." *Gambling.Net*, 2024, www.gambling.net/history/.

Gavrilovic, Dejan. "Psychology of Gambling, MBTI, and Seven Types of Players." *Latest Casino Bonuses*, Latest Casino Bonuses, 17 Jan. 2022, lcb.org/news/editorials/the-mindset-of-luck-choices-and-balances.

Grimes, Stephanie. "Knowing Vegas: What's the Story behind Nevada's Black Book?" *Las Vegas Review Journal*, Las Vegas Review-Journal, 23 June 2017, www.reviewjournal.com/uncategorized/knowing-vegas-whats-the-story-behind-nevadas-black-book/.

Groette, Oddmund. "Van K. Tharp – the Psychology of Trading Mastery - Quantified Trading Strategies." *Quantified Strategies*, 12 Feb. 2024, www.quantifiedstrategies.com/ van-k-tharp/.

Hernandez, Daisy. "Senet Board Game | How Did This Ancient Egyptian Board Game Work?" *Ancient Egyptians Had Their Own Kind of Ouija Board*, 11 Feb. 2022, www.popularmechanics.com/culture/gaming/a30795404/ ancient-egyptian-game-senet/.

"Home Page." National Council on Problem Gambling, 5 Mar. 2024, www.ncpgambling.org/.

Ivanovska, Elena. "The History of US Gambling - a Complete Timeline." *History of US Gambling*, 28 Apr. 2023, time2play.com/blog/history-of-us-gambling.

Ivany, Roderick, et al. "Cooking up Luck - Gastronomic Superstitions and Rituals in Gambling - Fatty Crab." *Fatty Crab* ◈, 6 Jan. 2024, www.fattycrab.com/cooking-up-luck-gastronomic-superstitions-and-rituals-in-gambling/.

Manolo. "8 Historical Figures That Studied Numerology." *Better Numerology*, 22 Jan. 2022, www.betternumerology.com/8-historical-figures-that-studied-numerology/.

Mitrovic, Milka. "Gambling Superstitions (2019) | Bad Luck Numbers - Askgamblers." *Gambling Superstitions*, AskGamblers.com, 11 July 2019, www.askgamblers.com/ gambling-news/blog/gambling-superstitions/.

"Mrs. L. Dow Balliett." Edited by Early History of Atlantic County, New Jersey: Record of the First Year's work of Atlantic County's Historical Society (with Laura Lavinia Thomas Willis and Mrs. M. R. M. Fish; 1915), *Wikipedia*, Wikimedia

Foundation, 31 Jan. 2024, en.m.wikipedia.org/wiki/Mrs._L._Dow_Balliett.

Numeros, Ethan. "5 Best Numerologists in the World." *Digits Mystic*, 12 Sept. 2023, digitsmystic.com/numerology/numerologists/.

Odonohoe, Rhiannon. "Most Superstitious Fan Bases across Major Professional Sports Leagues." *Casino.Org Blog*, 17 Jan. 2024, www.casino.org/blog/superstitious-fans-leagues/.

Pollux, Amaria. "10 Powerful Money Herbs and How to Use Them." *WiccaNow*, 14 Sept. 2023, wiccanow.com/top-10-most-powerfull-money-herbs-and-how-to-use-them/.

Priory, Mount Grace. "Significance of Mount Grace Priory." *English Heritage*, www.english-heritage.org.uk/visit/places/mount-grace-priory/history-and-stories/history/significance/. Accessed 19 Feb. 2024.

Public Broadcast Service, PBS. "Nova Online | Trillion Dollar Bet | the Formula That Shook the World." *PBS*, Public Broadcasting Service, 2000, www.pbs.org/wgbh/nova/stockmarket/formula.html.

Singapore, National Library Board. *Gambling Farms in the 19th Century*, 9 Oct. 2023, www.nlb.gov.sg/main/article-detail?cmsuuid=a120b925-44c0-49d8-af19-9f475c536f64.

Sohn, Emily. "How Gambling Affects the Brain and Who Is Most Vulnerable to Addiction." *Monitor on Psychology*, American Psychological Association, 1 July 2023, www.apa.org/monitor/2023/07/how-gambling-affects-the-brain.

Sun, Palm Beach. "Every Name in the Las Vegas Black Book." *Every Name in the Las Vegas Black Book Here They Are, All the People Who Are Not Allowed in a Vegas Casino*, 2024, palmbeachsun.net/EVERY-NAME-IN-THE-LAS-VEGAS-BLACK-BOOK——-Here-they-are%2C-all-the-people-who-are-not-allowed-in-a-Vegas-Casino.

Team, The Numerologist. "The History of Numerology." *Numerologist.Com*, 25 May 2021, numerologist.com/numerology/the-history-of-numerology/.

Templar, Admin-. "Eliphas Levi: The Man behind Baphomet." *Templar History*, 17 July 2023, templarhistory.com/eliphas-levi-the-man-behind-baphomet/.

This is a partial list of written works of Papus (Gérard Encausse) including works in French. "Gérard Encausse." *Wikipedia*, Wikimedia Foundation, 1 Feb. 2024, en.m.wikipedia.org/wiki/G%C3%A9rard_Encausse.

Tormsen, David. "10 Folk Magic Traditions of the Early Modern Era." *Listverse*, 17 Nov. 2015, listverse.com/2015/11/17/10-folk-magic-traditions-of-the-early-modern-era/.

Twofeathers, Shirley. "Herbs for Luck." *Magickal Ingredients*, 24 Apr. 2015, shirleytwofeathers.com/The_Blog/magickal-ingredients/herbs-for-luck/.

Tyler, Mara. "Gambling Addiction: Symptoms, Causes, and Treatment." Healthline, Healthline Media, 17 Dec. 2016, www.healthline.com/health/addiction/gambling#resources.

Velotta, Richard N. "Las Vegas Man Becomes 35th Person Added to Nevada's Black Book." *Journal*, Las Vegas Review-Journal, 21 Dec. 2018, www.reviewjournal.com/business/casinos-gaming/las-vegas-man-becomes-35th-person-added-to-nevadas-black-book-1555896/.

"What Games Did the Ancient Egyptians Play?" *BBC Bitesize*, BBC, 2024, www.bbc.co.uk/bitesize/topics/zg87xnb/articles/z4wdnrd.

Wigington, Patti. "Hoodoo in American Folk Magic." *Learn Religions*, Learn Religions, 5 July 2019, www.learnreligions.com/what-is-hoodoo-2561899.

Wikipedia, Foundation. "Augustine of Hippo." *Wikipedia*, Wikimedia Foundation, 18 Feb. 2024, en.m.wikipedia.org/wiki/Augustine_of_Hippo.

Wikipedia, Foundation. "Pythagoras." *Wikipedia*, Wikimedia Foundation, 18 Feb. 2024, en.m.wikipedia.org/wiki/Pythagoras.

Wintle, Simon. "Early History of Playing Cards & Timeline." *The World of Playing Cards*, www.wopc.co.uk/the-history-of-playing-cards/early-history-of-playing-cards. Accessed 19 Feb. 2024.

Wood, Will, et al. "The Trillion Dollar Equation." *Veritasium*, YouTube, 27 Feb. 2024, www.youtube.com/watch?v=A5w-dEgIU1M.

Writer, Casino.org Staff. "The History of Luck Charms, Amulets, and Superstition." *Casino.Org Blog*, 5 Feb. 2024, www.casino.org/blog/the-history-of-luck-charms-amulets-and-superstition/.

Yronwode, Cathrine. *The Evil Eye*, 1999, www.luckymojo.com/evileye.html.

Yu, A. Z., et al. (2016). Pantheon 1.0, a manually verified dataset of globally famous biographies. Scientific Data 2:150075. doi: 10.1038/sdata.2015.75. "Gérard Encausse Biography - Physician, Hypnotist, Occultist Reformer of Martinism." *Pantheon*, 2015, pantheon.world/profile/person/Gérard_Encausse.

# About the Author

Georgia Liberty is a wife, mother and witch living and communing with nature in rural Georgia while writing about the magickal realm of the world in her spare time. Georgia has been a practicing witch for 20 years and Mr. Big's Magickal Guide to Gambling is her premiere guide for readers to gain an introduction to magickal gambling strategies. Her unique perspective that draws from her personal knowledge of studying the craft for two decades brings a strong entry level foundation to the concept of incorporating magick into gambling strategies. Georgia begins the manual by enticing the imagination with the potential possibilities to draw extra luck and prosperity to a gambling enterprise, but at the end, she instinctively includes resource materials for individuals seeking specific rites, or rituals, and for those seeking help with gambling addictions. Her reflection upon the entire arena of gaming culture from a magickal perspective gives the entire book, Mr. Big's Magickal Guide to Gambling, a rounded, thoughtful construction from beginning to end.

The Co-Author on this work Wayne Clingman, otherwise known as Mr. Big himself, is a author and book contributor best known for his crime documentary works such as, The Life and Times of Frank Balistrieri: The Last, Most Powerful Godfather of Milwaukee, and The Buffalo Mob: The Return Of Organized Crime To The Queen City both available on Amazon. Wayne lives with his wife, cats and dogs in Wisconsin and has been publishing works about real crime, mob tactics and lifestyles since 2019. His personal extension of lived practical advice invested in his book, Mr. Big's Magickal Guide to Gambling, illustrates the manners in which magick can be implemented into different variations of gambling methods.

https://rumble.com/user/WiccanConservative
https://twitter.com/LibertyWiccan
http://www.youtube.com/@wiccanconservative
https://twitter.com/Milwaukeemob2
https://www.amazon.com/dp/b0bd2l4cyg

Milton Keynes UK
Ingram Content Group UK Ltd.
UKHW011108180424
441376UK00001B/14